P9-EJZ-300

"Hulk SMASH!" adapted by Clarissa Wong. Illustrated Ron Lim and Rachelle Rosenberg. Based on the Marvel comic book series *The Avengers*.

"Black Widow Bites Back!" adapted by Elizabeth Schaefer. Illustrated by Neil Edwards and Rachelle Rosenberg. Based on the Marvel comic book series *The Avengers*.

"Friend or Foe?" adapted by Alison Lowenstein. Illustrated by Khoi Pham and Paul Mounts. Based on the Marvel comic book series *The Avengers*.

"Falcon Earns His Wings" written by Scott Peterson. Illustrated by Andrea Di Vito and Rachelle Rosenberg. Based on the Marvel comic book series *The Avengers*.

"Party Crashers" written by Michael Siglain. Illustrated by Neil Edwards and Rachelle Rosenberg. Based on the Marvel comic book series *The Avengers*.

"Battle for Earth!" written by Patrick Olliffe. Illustrated by Khoi Pham and Paul Mounts. Based on the Marvel comic book series *The Avengers*.

"Arctic Attack!" written by Frank Bumbalo. Illustrated by Khoi Pham and Paul Mounts. Based on the Marvel comic book series *The Avengers*.

"Kang—Conqueror of S.H.I.E.L.D.!" written by Bryan Q. Miller. Illustrated by Neil Edwards and Rachelle Rosenberg. Based on the Marvel comic book series *The Avengers*.

"Call for Backup" written by Chris "Doc" Wyatt. Illustrated by Khoi Pham and Paul Mounts. Based on the Marvel comic book series *The Avengers*.

"Hail, Hydra!" written by Alison Lowenstein. Illustrated by Wellinton Alvez and Paul Mounts. Based on the Marvel comic book series *The Avengers*.

"Attack of Count Nefaria" written by Alison Lowenstein. Illustrated by Andrea Di Vito and Paul Mounts. Based on the Marvel comic book series *The Avengers*.

"Play Ball!" written by Scott Peterson. Illustrated by Agustin Padilla and Rachelle Rosenberg. Based on the Marvel comic book series *The Avengers*.

"Thor Versus the Avengers" written by Rebecca Schmidt. Illustrated by Wellinton Alvez and Rachelle Rosenberg. Based on the Marvel comic book series *The Avengers*.

"Double Take" written by Ivan Cohen. Illustrated by Andrea Di Vito and Rachelle Rosenberg. Based on the Marvel comic book series *The Avengers*.

"Jurassic Central Park" written by Tomas Palacios. Illustrated by Agustin Padilla and Rachelle Rosenberg. Based on the Marvel comic book series *The Avengers*.

"The Avengers' Day Off" written by Alison Lowenstein. Illustrated by Neil Edwards and Rachelle Rosenberg. Based on the Marvel comic book series *The Avengers*.

"Undercover Agents" written by Colin Hosten. Illustrated by Andrea Di Vito and Rachelle Rosenberg. Based on the Marvel comic book series *The Avengers*.

"What Goes Up Must Come Down" written by Ivan Cohen. Illustrated by Agustin Padilla and Rachelle Rosenberg. Based on the Marvel comic book series *The Avengers*.

"An Unexpected Hero" written by Chris "Doc" Wyatt. Illustrated by Neil Edwards and Rachelle Rosenberg. Based on the Marvel comic book series *The Avengers*.

Cover illustrated by Ron Lim, Khoi Pham, Andrea Di Vito, Drew Geraci, Paul Mounts and Pete Pantazis.

marvelkids.com

For information address Marvel Press, 125 West End Avenue, New York, New York 10023.

Printed in the United States of America

First Hardcover Edition, March 2015
10 9 8 7 6 5 4 3 2

FAC-038091-6-15219

Library of Congress
Control Number:
2014944497

ISBN 978-1-4847-0242-0

Hulk SMASH!

Hulk is one of Earth's Mightiest Heroes. No one could deny his incredible strength or size. Whether fighting alone or side by side with the Avengers, he can take down almost any villain. Even villains as huge as he is are no problem! But before he became the incredible Hulk, he was just a man named Bruce Banner.

Bruce is a brilliant scientist. Before he became Hulk, he spent his time studying a special kind of energy called gamma radiation. Bruce knew the gamma rays were dangerous, but he wanted to show the world that they could be used for good.

Bruce decided that the best way to test the gamma rays' power was to set up an explosion. Then he could measure the radiation they gave off.

Bruce carefully set up a testing site in the middle of the desert. He knew he needed to do his test in an empty place so no one would get hurt. But something terrible happened! A young boy wandered right into the testing area.

Jumping into his car, Bruce raced off to save the boy.

Bruce arrived at the test site with only moments to spare! He grabbed the boy and threw him into a nearby bomb shelter. But Bruce was not so lucky. Before he could get himself to safety, his device exploded.

Bruce woke up in an army hospital. The army had found him in the desert. They were worried about him.

Bruce looked at himself in the mirror. He didn't feel sick, but he did feel . . . different.

Suddenly, Bruce felt something strange. His head hurt and he let out a loud cry. Bruce looked down in shock. His skin was starting to turn green! His hands expanded and his muscles grew until he was four times his normal size!

Bruce knew the radiation from the blast was to blame, but he was powerless to stop the change that had come over him. In a fit of anger, Bruce smashed through the brick wall of the hospital and escaped. Some nearby soldiers saw him and yelled into their radios: Look out for a green monster, a Goliath, a HULK!

All Hulk wanted was to be left alone. He did not want to hurt anyone. But the army could not let the mysterious monster escape. A tank full of soldiers chased after him! The soldiers surrounded Hulk.

As the tank fired at Hulk, a rush of rage came over the green beast. He clenched his fists and roared, "HULK SMASH!"

Hulk easily lifted the large tank and threw it across the field. Then, before the fighting could start again, he leaped away. He did not want to fight.

Hulk ran until the soldiers were out of sight. When he was safely away, he tried to calm down.

As his anger eased, he felt his body change again. He became smaller, and the green left his skin. Soon he was Bruce Banner once more.

Bruce wanted to keep the truth about Hulk a secret. He hoped he would never become Hulk again. But Hulk was not gone. Every time Bruce felt angry or frustrated, he transformed into Hulk.

Bruce tried to remain calm at all times, but when he saw Super Villains hurting innocent people, he could not stay calm. He wanted to defend the helpless. So did Hulk!

The problem was, people were scared of Hulk. They pointed and called him a monster.

This made Hulk sad. He thought that if he kept helping people, maybe they would realize he was friendly. But no matter how hard he tried, people still ran from him.

Slowly, Bruce realized that people who judged Hulk on his appearance were wrong!

Hulk knew that he could do great things for others. He could fight for those in trouble and save people from danger. The green Goliath was very powerful, and he wanted to use that power for good!

No matter how big or small the problem, Hulk was there to save the day. Hulk was a big hero with a big heart. The more good he did, the more people came to love him.

But there are times when a threat is too big for any one hero to handle, and so Hulk became part of the mighty team of Avengers. Now he stands proud among Captain America, Iron Man, Thor, Falcon, Black Widow, and Hawkeye. Together, Hulk and the Avengers fight for the good of the world—just like Bruce Banner always wanted!

Black Widow Bites Back!

Natasha Romanoff and her brother, Alexi, were orphans. The two had been raised at an orphanage known as the Red Room.

The Red Room was really home to a secret Russian spy program.

Natasha and Alexi were spies. Together they went on missions to gather information about S.H.I.E.L.D. The two had just failed their most recent assignment. Now they were waiting outside the office of the Red Room's leader, Ivan Bezukhov.

"This is all my fault," Alexi said. "Every time we've failed, it's been because of something I messed up."

"Don't worry," Natasha replied. "I'll take care of you." But Natasha *was* worried. They had made too many mistakes lately, and Ivan was *not* a patient man.

"You're so good at this spy stuff, Natasha," Alexi told his sister. "You're like a black widow. I'm like a clumsy hippo, ruining everything."

"Natasha." Ivan's voice came from behind them. "I'll see you in my office now. Alone."

Natasha gave Alexi a reassuring smile, then stepped into Ivan's office.

"Today was not a good day for you, the Red Room, or—most importantly—me," Ivan said coldly. "Alexi has been the cause of too many failed missions. He must be disposed of."

"No!" Natasha cried.

Natasha knew that the Red Room disposed of failed spies by erasing their memories.

"If you erase his memory, he won't remember who *I* am," Natasha said. She knew she couldn't allow that to happen.

Natasha ran from Ivan's office. She was too late. Red Room agents were already dragging her brother away.

Natasha fought her way to freedom. She would find a way to rescue Alexi. She had to!

Natasha went to the only people she knew could help—her old enemy, S.H.I.E.L.D. Using her spy gear from the Red Room, Natasha reprogrammed an old S.H.I.E.L.D. ID badge to fool the security guards. Then, disguised as a janitor, she snuck into S.H.I.E.L.D. headquarters.

Natasha casually walked past the guard. Once he was out of sight, she slipped into an air vent.

A few twists and turns later, Natasha was directly above Director Nick Fury's office. Natasha flipped down onto Fury's desk. He was shocked! Before Fury could call security, Natasha asked him for his help—and his forgiveness.

"I know I've caused a lot of trouble for your team," Natasha told Fury, "but I'll do anything S.H.I.E.L.D. asks if you help me rescue my brother."

Fury reluctantly agreed. Natasha and Alexi *had* caused a lot of trouble, but he couldn't leave Alexi to the mercy of the Red Room.

Fury introduced Natasha to the Avengers. Natasha was surprised at how willing they were to help even though none of them knew her.

"We'll rescue your brother," Captain America promised.

"Taking on the Red Room will be tricky, even for a super spy like you, Natasha," Tony Stark said. "I think you need some upgraded tech!"

That evening, Natasha led the Avengers to the Red Room's secret base. The Avengers freed Ivan's prisoners as they searched for Alexi.

Suddenly, Natasha heard a familiar voice behind her say, "I see you've come home." It was Ivan! The leader of the Red Room threw a punch at Natasha.

"Where is my brother?" Natasha asked, fighting Ivan off.

Ivan laughed as he blocked her every move.

“You can’t hurt me,” Ivan said.

“*I* can’t, but I bet *this* will.” Natasha fired a powerful electric blast from her gauntlet, knocking Ivan to the ground.

“What was that?” Ivan cried.

“An upgrade from Tony Stark. Now, where is my brother?”

Ivan knew he couldn’t fight against the Avengers’ technology. He told Natasha where to find Alexi.

Natasha rushed to Alexi's cell. His eyes were closed and he looked weak.

"Alexi," she called.

Alexi's eyes fluttered. "What—what are you doing here? I thought Ivan got rid of you . . ." he said.

"You're okay!" Natasha shouted, hugging her brother.

Natasha smiled up at the Avengers. She knew she couldn't have saved Alexi without them.

Later, back at S.H.I.E.L.D. headquarters, Nick Fury took Natasha aside. “I don’t know many spies who would have been able to break into my office. Or who would risk their lives for someone else,” he said. “I would like you to join Earth’s mightiest team of Super Heroes, the Avengers. What do you say, Natasha?”

“Count me in!” Natasha said with a smile. “You can call me Black Widow.”

Friend or Foe?

Clint Barton and his brother, Barney, grew up in an orphanage. Life was not always easy for the brothers, but at least they had each other. One of their favorite things to do was make up stories about being Super Heroes. The two spent hours at the playground wearing capes and masks and pretending to save the world from villains.

When they were older, the boys left the orphanage and set out to explore the world. On their travels, they passed a traveling circus. It piqued their interest.

"Remember how we dreamed about joining the circus? This is our chance!" Clint said to his brother.

"Maybe they need help!" Barney exclaimed.

As it turned out, the circus *did* need workers.

The brothers quickly learned many jobs. Barney enjoyed helping out behind the curtain, while Clint took advantage of his skill with a bow and arrow to become a headlining act.

Clint's stage name was Hawkeye, the World's Greatest Marksman. He was the star performer!

Hawkeye's popularity made the circus very successful. People traveled from far away just to see his act.

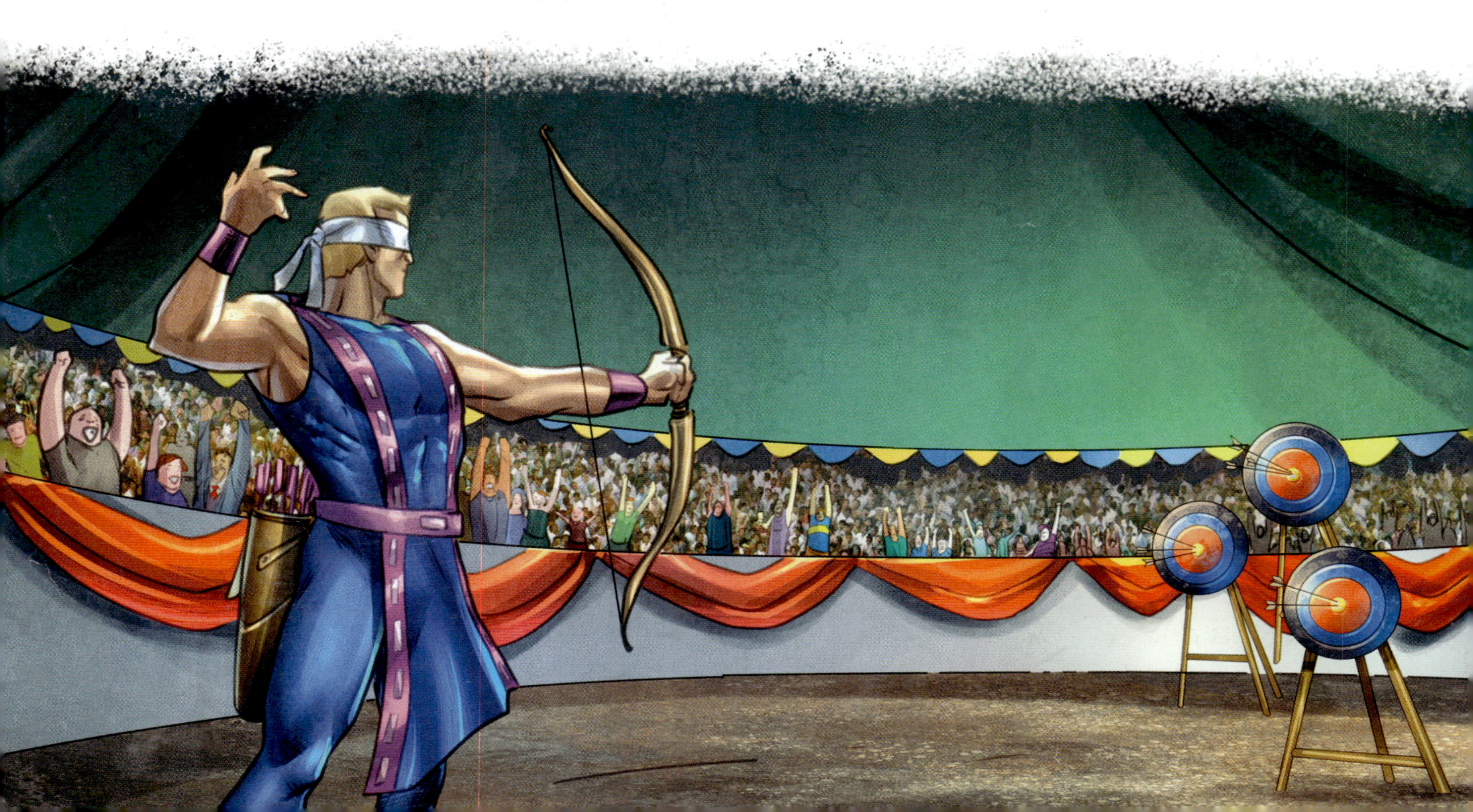

One night, Hawkeye saw a light on in the box office. He was shocked to see another performer, the Swordsman, stealing money.

"What are you doing?" asked Hawkeye.

The Swordsman pushed Hawkeye and ran off. Hawkeye aimed his arrow at the Swordsman, but he couldn't bring himself to hurt the thief.

The other people in the circus were upset that Hawkeye hadn't stopped the Swordsman. They asked him to leave.

With nowhere else to go, Hawkeye started performing at a beachfront carnival. One day, an explosion rocked the roller coaster. The riders were stuck on it and in danger of falling off. Hawkeye wanted to help.

Looking at the sky, Hawkeye saw a red-and-gold streak. It was the invincible Iron Man!

The armored Avenger had arrived just in time to catch the falling ride and help the riders to safety.

Watching Iron Man, Hawkeye realized that he wanted to help people, too.

That night, Hawkeye made a costume of his own. He also created a variety of special arrows.

"I'm not just Hawkeye the performer," he said as he sewed the last stitches on his costume. "I'm Hawkeye the Super Hero."

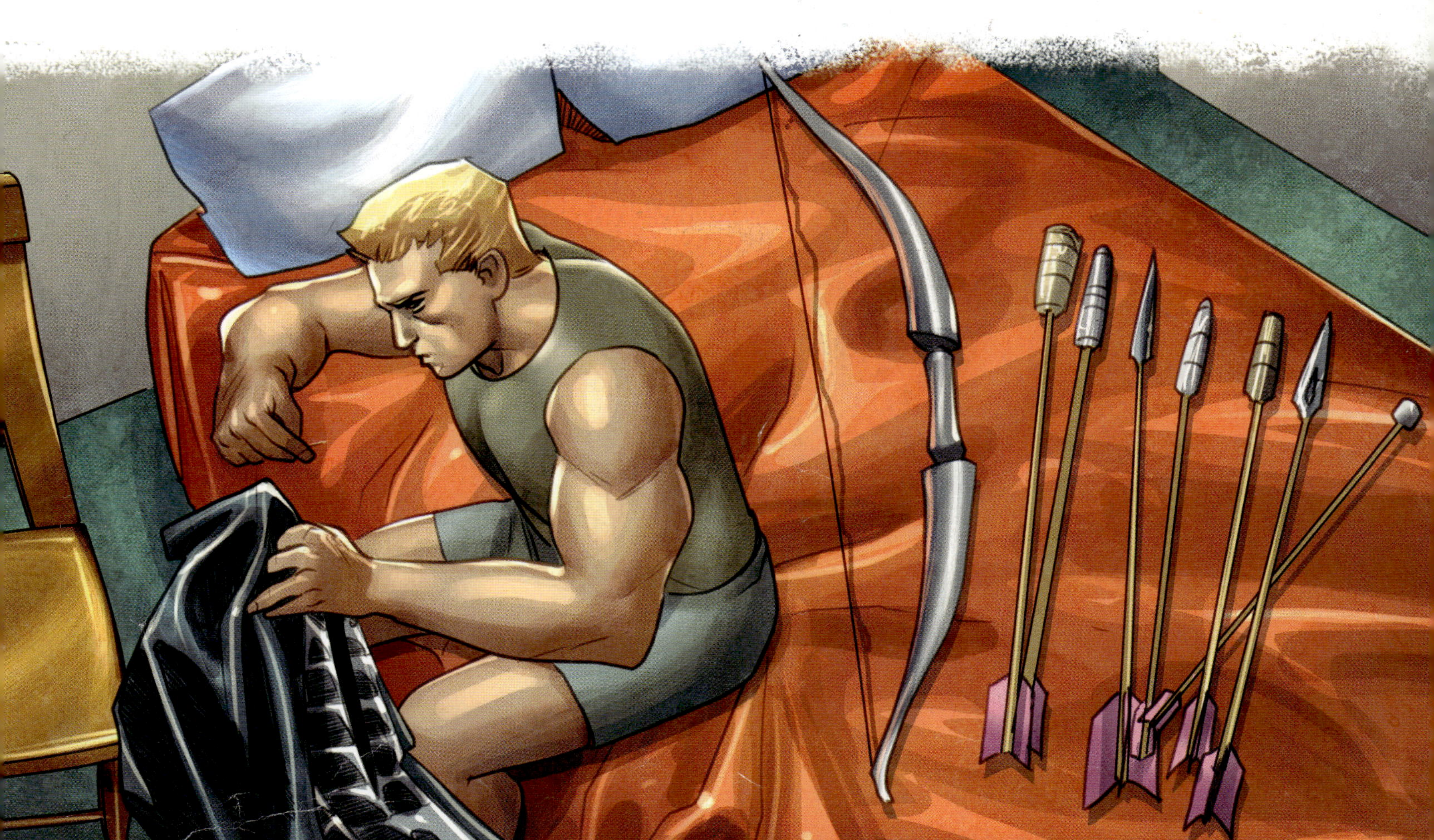

The next day, Hawkeye was walking past a jewelry store when an alarm went off. A moment later, a man ran out carrying a bag.

This was Hawkeye's chance! He pointed his bow at the thief, who dropped the bag and fled.

Hawkeye picked up the bag to take it back into the store. Just then, the police surrounded him. They thought *he* was the robber!

Suddenly, Iron Man appeared. He thought Hawkeye was guilty, too!

Iron Man fired a repulsor ray at Hawkeye, but the archer was too fast! He jumped out of the way and shot an arrow at the Super Hero. The arrow bounced off Iron Man's armor and exploded in a puff of smoke.

Now Iron Man was getting angry. He fired another blast at Hawkeye, and again Hawkeye jumped out of the way.

Hawkeye quickly grabbed an arrow from his quiver and fired an electrified net at the Avenger. Iron Man was trapped!

Hawkeye knew he had only seconds to explain himself.

"I don't want to fight!" he said. "I'm not the jewel thief. I was trying to stop the thief. I want to be a Super Hero like you."

Just then, the other Avengers arrived. Hawkeye knew he couldn't fight them all, and he surrendered.

"Wait," Iron Man commanded. "Don't hurt this man. He's innocent. I just heard over my armor's radio that the police have caught the real thief."

Hawkeye helped Iron Man out of the net, and the two heroes shook hands.

"You did a great job today," Iron Man said. "I want you to meet the Avengers. I think you'd make a great addition to our team."

Hawkeye could hardly believe it. His childhood dream had come true. Not only was he a Super Hero—he was now one of the mighty Avengers!

Falcon Earns His Wings

alcon.

An invaluable member of the Avengers.

One of Captain America's best friends.

A brave hero who has saved the lives of Iron Man, Thor, and Hulk.

But he hasn't always been this way.

Once upon a time, Falcon was just a boy named Sam Wilson.

Young Sam grew up in a tough part of New York City. His parents did their best to love him, protect him, and teach him right from wrong.

Sam had always felt a close connection with birds. His parents encouraged his love of animals. They even let him keep a pigeon coop on the roof of their apartment building.

But Sam lost his parents at an early age. Feeling hurt, scared, and helpless, Sam decided the only way to survive was to become tougher and harder than anyone else.

Soon that was exactly what Sam was—tough! He did what it took to get ahead. But he always made sure to do what was right and stand up for others who felt as helpless as he once had.

To get a break from the city, Sam took a job on a strange island called the Isle of Exiles. But when he arrived, Sam discovered the island had been taken over by the evil Red Skull and his Hydra army!

Red Skull imprisoned Sam. He wanted him to work for Hydra. Sam managed to get away, but not before Red Skull gave him the ability to communicate with birds.

Sam didn't run far. He realized that there might be other people on the island who were being forced to work for Hydra. Sam decided to go back and free them! But he couldn't do it alone.

Sam was trying to devise a plan when he heard a noise coming from the jungle. He followed the sound and found a falcon trapped in a cage. The bird was not hurt, but it was unable to free itself. Sam immediately felt a bond with the falcon and released it.

Sam named the falcon Redwing. He prepared a message and told the bird to take it to anyone it could find.

Soon enough, Redwing returned with Captain America! When Sam told Cap of Red Skull's evil plans, the two decided to team up against Hydra.

But Sam would need to gear up for such a dangerous mission. Captain America called S.H.I.E.L.D. agent Phil Coulson, who delivered a special suit for Sam.

Falcon was born!

Along with Captain America and Redwing, he snuck deep into the Isle of Exiles and freed the other prisoners.

Hydra was strong and powerful, but it was no match for such a mighty team. Even Red Skull's Cosmic Cube, which allowed him to bend the fabric of reality, could not save the Super Villain.

Together, the heroes defeated Cap's most dangerous enemy.

Sam knew it was time to return to New York. He could not run from his pain. He had to face it.

But Sam was not the scared boy he had once been. As Falcon, he could help make New York a safer place.

Falcon often partnered with Captain America. S.H.I.E.L.D. even made him a set of artificial wings that enabled him to fly.

Now Sam really was like a falcon.

Falcon proved himself time and again. Eventually, he was even asked to join the Avengers.

Earth's Mightiest Heroes gained a strong, resourceful new member.

And Falcon found a new family at last.

MARVEL
THE
AVENGERS
Party Crashers

Billionaire inventor and scientist Tony Stark—better known as Iron Man—was hosting the annual Stark Expo. Scientists from around the world had gathered at his offices in New York City to unveil their latest inventions. This was their chance to show the scientific community what they had been working on.

Tony was leading the conference, but he was not alone. He had brought the Avengers with him. Tony knew that so much technology in one place was sure to attract attention, and he wanted to make sure that none of the scientists—or their inventions—fell into the wrong hands.

"With so many brilliant people working together," Tony Stark told his guests, "I know that we can make the world a better place. And so I would like to—"

Suddenly, Tony was interrupted by a booming voice at the other end of the hall: "These scientists—and their inventions—now belong to the Masters of Evil!"

The scientists gasped and turned around. Standing across the room were four of the most dangerous Super Villains in the world: Baron Zemo, Ultron, the Enchantress, and Klaw. Each one was tough—but when they worked together as the Masters of Evil, they were almost unstoppable.

Captain America sprang into action. The Super Hero launched himself at Baron Zemo, knocking him back with his unbreakable vibranium shield.

“Tony—suit up!” Cap yelled. Then, turning to the rest of his team, he cried, “Avengers, ASSEMBLE!”

Tony called his Iron Man armor to him. The pieces flew through the air and attached themselves to his body. Iron Man wasted no time. Firing his repulsors, he blasted a hole in the side of the wall for the scientists to escape through. But before he could yell to them, a high-pitched sound blasted through the expo.

Klaw was using sound waves to stop the scientists from escaping. The high-pitched waves caused them to fall to the ground in pain.

Iron Man had heard enough. "Can you play any other tunes?" he asked. Iron Man fired a repulsor blast at Klaw that sent him crashing to the ground, and the horrible sound stopped.

On the other side of the expo, the Enchantress rose into the air. Looking around the room, she quickly focused her attention on a group of frightened scientists.

The Enchantress laughed. She knew that her magic was powerful, but with the help of the scientists' technology, she would be *unstoppable*!

Lifting her hand, the Enchantress fired an energy blast at the scientists. But her powers were blocked by Thor and his mighty hammer, Mjolnir! The energy bounced off the hammer and rebounded back at the Enchantress.

"Get thee off Midgard!" the Asgardian warrior yelled.

The Enchantress laughed again and created a protective shield around herself. The shield deflected the energy, leaving her unharmed. "I will leave Earth only with these scientists as my prisoners!" she hissed.

"Not today!" a voice yelled from behind. It was Black Widow!

The Enchantress's protective shield may have been powerful against magic, but it could not stop pure physical force. Black Widow delivered a powerful blow to the unsuspecting villainess, knocking her out cold.

With the villain out of the way, Black Widow turned to see where else she could be of help.

Across the room, the scientists ran for the exit. But they did not get far. Ultron and his terrible robots were blocking the way.

Black Widow tried to get to the scientists, but there were too many robots.

"Hawkeye!" she called.

Hawkeye lifted a special electric arrow from his quiver and fired it at one of the robots, causing it to short out.

"Get to the other exit," he yelled to the scientists.

The scientists fled to the other side of the room . . . all but one.

Dr. Bruce Banner stood beside Hawkeye, taking in the situation around him.

"You know," Hawkeye called over his shoulder as he drew and fired another arrow, "we could really use the big guy's help right now."

Bruce nodded. It was a good thing these robots were making him angry!

Focusing his energy, Bruce let his rage flow freely. Suddenly, his hands and feet began to grow bigger. His shoulders grew wider and his shirt tore off his back.

Bruce let out an angry roar. But he wasn't Bruce anymore. He was the incredible Hulk!

"Hulk smash!" Hulk roared. With a mighty swing of his arm, he knocked over three of Ultron's robots.

Ultron was not going down without a fight. Raising his arms, he commanded his robotic army to attack Hulk.

The robots charged and blasted Hulk. It looked like the green Goliath was outmatched—until Iron Man, Falcon, and Thor joined the fight.

"You're the perfect example of technology gone bad," Iron Man yelled to Ultron as he fired one repulsor blast after another.

“On the contrary, I am the perfect example of technology!” the villain replied. And as his robotic minions attacked the Avengers, Ultron snuck off to rejoin the other Masters of Evil.

Baron Zemo, Ultron, Klaw, and the Enchantress regrouped in the center of the expo. “The Avengers are formidable adversaries,” Baron Zemo began. “If they will not let us leave with the scientists, then we will destroy the entire expo. Prepare for our escape—I will set the explosives!”

"Not so fast!" a voice yelled behind them. The villains turned. Much to their surprise, they saw the scientists—and their technology—blocking their escape.

"You're not going anywhere," a familiar voice called out from the opposite side of the room. It was Captain America and the Avengers. The Super Heroes and the scientists had the Super Villains surrounded. There was nowhere left for them to go, and nothing left for them to do but surrender!

After S.H.I.E.L.D. took away the Masters of Evil, the Stark Expo started over and Iron Man addressed the crowd. "Our future depends on science and technology. And with all of us working together—like we just did today—I know that we can make the world a better place. And I know that the Avengers—and all of you—will always be there to protect it!"

Battle for Earth!

It was a quiet night. The Avengers were enjoying a well-deserved rest when an explosion rocked the Natural History Museum.

The Avengers arrived at the scene to see Thanos—one of the galaxy's most dangerous villains!

Thanos was looking for an ancient artifact—the magical Sword of Histria.

The Super Villain fired a blast of energy at Captain America using his Infinity Gauntlet, a magic glove that drew its energy from six powerful gems.

Captain America quickly raised his indestructible shield. But Thanos was very powerful. The force of his blast threw Captain America backward into his fellow Avenger, Falcon.

"You humans are no match for me," the villain bellowed as he moved deeper into the museum. "Once I have the Sword of Histria, I will slice your beloved planet Earth in two!"

Hawkeye moved into position to stop the Super Villain, but Thanos was faster than the hero had imagined. Before Hawkeye could even lift his bow, Thanos spun around and blasted the archer off his feet!

Turning back around, Thanos smashed the glass case that protected the Sword of Histria.

Thanos laughed as he took hold of the magical artifact.

"The Sword is mine!" he roared triumphantly. "My plan is almost complete! No one will be able to stop me now!"

Captain America and Black Widow charged toward Thanos, but they were too late.

With an evil laugh, the Super Villain teleported away with the Sword, leaving Cap and Black Widow to look after an injured Hawkeye and Falcon.

High above the ground, hidden among the clouds, hovered the massive S.H.I.E.L.D. Helicarrier, headquarters of the world's best super spies.

On board, the Avengers met with Nick Fury, the director of S.H.I.E.L.D.

“We know why Thanos stole the Sword of Histria and what his ultimate plan is,” Captain America told the group. “What we don’t know is where he’s going.”

“According to intel on the Sword, it’s powerless unless it’s returned to the place it was created,” Iron Man said.

Nick Fury shook his head. “That could be anywhere.”

Just then, Special Agent Ruby, who specialized in ancient artifacts, joined the group.

"Maybe I can help," Agent Ruby said. "The Sword was being held for safekeeping at the Natural History Museum, but my sources say it was created at Castle Aarole in the Carpathian Mountains."

Agent Ruby pulled up an image of the castle.

Nick Fury looked at the image, then turned to the group. "Looks like you're going to Romania."

The Avengers wasted no time. They boarded the Quinjet and raced to Romania!

The heroes soon arrived at Castle Aarole. But Thanos had beaten them there. As the Avengers rushed toward him, the Sword of Histria began to glow with ancient energy. It was very close to the place it had been forged!

The Avengers had to stop Thanos, and fast. They were the planet's last hope! They sprang into action, but Thanos wasn't going down without a fight.

Thor and Hulk pressed the attack! While Thor threw his enchanted hammer, Mjolnir, at Thanos, Hulk smashed his fists into the ground. Shock waves radiated out, shaking the earth. But Thanos had drawn extra energy from the Sword of Histria. He was now more powerful than ever! He easily deflected Thor's hammer and withstood Hulk's shock waves.

As the Sword pulsed with magical energy, Thanos stepped over the crumbled outer castle wall. Just a few more feet, and the Sword would be at full power.

Iron Man raced in to stop Thanos, but the Super Villain used the power of the Sword to short-circuit Iron Man's armor! As Thanos continued forward, he fired an energy blast at Hulk. Thanos knew the blast would only temporarily blind Hulk, but it would give him the time he needed.

With Hulk out of the way, Thanos swept past the rest of the Avengers and into the ancient castle.

Behind him, Black Widow fired electrostatic bolts from her bracelets. But she was too late! The energy had no effect on the Super Villain. Thanos had reached his destination—the very spot where the Sword of Histria had been created so many centuries earlier!

As Thanos raised the sword triumphantly in the air, a swirl of colorful lights appeared in the sky above him, temporarily blinding the Avengers. The blaze of energy engulfed Thanos and the mystical Sword.

The ground shook and cracked beneath the Avengers' feet. The air, charged with magical power, crackled around them! Had Thanos won?

The Avengers needed another plan!

Iron Man's armor was useless, but Tony Stark's genius-level mind was not! He had a plan. They couldn't defeat Thanos as long as he had the Sword. But they *could* destroy the Sword itself!

Thor used Mjolnir to call down the lightning and empower Captain America's shield with Asgardian energy.

Iron Man turned to Hulk. "We need your strength," he said.

At Iron Man's direction, Hulk hurled Cap's energized shield at the Sword of Histria.

Thanos, focused on the sword, did not realize that he was under attack. He was preparing to slice the earth in two when suddenly he saw a red, white, and blue blur zooming toward him. He could not react in time.

Captain America's shield, powered by Thor's Asgardian energy and the superhuman strength of the incredible Hulk, struck the Sword of Histria. Thanos managed to jump back, but he could not save the weapon. The magical artifact shattered into a thousand pieces.

The Sword's ancient energies were released, causing an enormous explosion that knocked Thanos back. Pieces of the sword fell to the ground around him.

Thanos knew he was defeated. His stolen sword was broken and his plans for the destruction of Earth were at an end.

The triumphant Avengers surrounded Thanos, but the Super Villain would not allow himself to be captured. As they closed in on him, Thanos teleported away!

The Avengers knew Thanos would return one day to finish what he'd started, and when he did, Earth's Mightiest Heroes would be there to stop him!

Arctic Attack!

The Avengers had just returned from a dangerous mission, but there would be no rest for this weary team of Super Heroes. Captain America had called a meeting to go over recent world events—much to the dismay of his tired teammates.

"Cap, can we speed this along?" Hawkeye yawned. The warm meeting room was making him tired. "If we're not going to be out there fighting bad guys, I'd like to get some rest."

"Have patience, Hawkeye," Captain America said. "You never know when we'll be needed—or where."

Suddenly, as if on cue, the Avengers' emergency alarm began to ring!

"Come in, Avengers. This is Matthew Woods from NORAD. I'm calling from the Arctic Ocean. We have an emergency! Can you hear me?"

"We hear you loud and clear, Matthew," Iron Man responded. "What's wrong?"

"It's the polar ice caps, Avengers," Matthew said. "There's something strange going on."

"Are they melting quicker than usual?" Falcon asked.

"No—just the opposite," Matthew said. "The ice is spreading at an extreme rate. If we don't stop it soon, it will engulf the northern hemisphere. The world is in grave danger."

The Avengers knew there wasn't a moment to lose. They rushed to the Quinjet and set off for the Arctic Ocean. At the top of the world, the Avengers were shocked by what they saw. Mountains of ice were erupting from the Arctic!

"Get us on the ground—fast," Cap told Black Widow. But before she could react, the temperature outside the Quinjet suddenly dropped—and so did the Quinjet!

"Brace yourselves, Avengers!" Black Widow screamed as the Quinjet spun out of control. "We are coming in hot!"

Iron Man, Falcon, and Thor tried their best to right the Quinjet, but their powers were no match for the frigid ice storm, and the Quinjet crashed into a massive snowbank.

"What caused the temperature to drop so fast?" Falcon asked as the escape hatch opened.

"Not what, friend Falcon—who. Look to the tallest iceberg to find your answer," Thor replied.

Falcon and the rest of the Avengers looked up to see the Frost Giants of Jotunheim.

"The Jotuns are the villains behind this deadly ice!" Thor continued as lightning began to crackle all around him. "Steadfast, Avengers—they are vile creatures."

"Ah, the son of Odin. We have been waiting for you," said Laufey, king of the Jotuns.

Laufey's eyes were as cold and blue as the frozen sky above, and he spoke with a voice that shook the very ground on which the heroes stood. "How do you like the work we are doing to your precious Midgard?" he continued.

Thor tightened his grip on his hammer, Mjolnir. "Laufey, cease your actions at once and return to Jotunheim," he said through gritted teeth. "I shall not warn you again."

"We shall not be returning, Odinson. Earth will be our home now," Laufey said as the ice and snow swirled around him. "The Asgardians destroyed our world. Your father himself led the attack, and what Odin took from the Jotuns, we shall take from his son!"

The wind and snow suddenly intensified, making it hard for the Avengers to see and breathe. The Jotun twins, Lok and Hagen, took out their massive clubs and charged toward Thor.

"Avengers, assemble!" Captain America shouted.

The Avengers fought with all their might, but they were no match for the combined threat of the Frost Giants and the intense storm.

"Cap!" Iron Man yelled into his comlink. "I have a plan, but I have to get back to the Quinjet. Can you keep them distracted, then round them up when I give the signal?"

“Will do, but make it quick,” Captain America responded. “I don’t know how much longer we can hold them off—or survive in this ice storm!”

Iron Man flew into the Quinjet, signaling for Hulk to go with him. Hulk retreated to the jet while the Jotuns created more snow and ice around them.

"Hulk," Iron Man began. "I need you to rip out the cargo bay doors. They're made of aluminum, which is a great conductor of electricity."

As Hulk tugged the metal doors, Iron Man spoke into his comlink again. "Avengers, listen up. We have to round up the Jotuns. Get them close together so Hulk and I can wrap them in aluminum. Then it's Thor's turn to bring the thunder—and the lightning!"

As the rest of the Avengers put Iron Man's plan into action, Thor stamped Mjolnir on the ground and called down the lightning. Working together, the Avengers electrified the Jotuns, putting a stop to the swirling storm.

Defeated, the Frost Giants fell to the ground. “Thank you, friends,” Thor said to his teammates. “I will take the Jotuns to the dungeon of Asgard.” He called to Heimdall to open the Rainbow Bridge.

As the Rainbow Bridge opened up, Cap turned to a shivering Hawkeye. “Bet you wish you were in a warm meeting room now,” he said.

“I sure do!” Hawkeye replied. “I’ve had enough of the Jotuns—and enough snow—to last me a lifetime!”

Kang–Conqueror of S.H.I.E.L.D.!

Kang was bored. He was a conqueror, but the thirty-first century had nothing left to conquer. He had conquered Earth. He had conquered the moon. He had even conquered the common cold!

Kang sighed. "I look upon my kingdom, and I weep, for I have no more worlds to conquer. No more rulers to overthrow or lands to—"

Suddenly, Kang grew quiet. He had just come up with the most delightfully sinister idea he'd ever had: he could travel back in time and conquer the world—all over again!

Kang laughed triumphantly.

"Once again, Kang will conquer all!" the Super Villain yelled.

Meanwhile, in the twenty-first century, S.H.I.E.L.D. agent Maria Hill was excited. The Avengers had been fighting more villains than usual lately. That meant Maria and her crew had been too busy to do all the odd jobs needed to keep her department running smoothly. Now, with the Avengers away on a longer mission, she finally had time to do some much-needed maintenance on the S.H.I.E.L.D. Helicarrier.

"Seize the day, gentlemen," Maria shouted. "We don't get many quiet moments around here. Let's use this time to clear the backlog of reports we have to write and make sure the engines are in tip-top shape."

Maria looked around and shuddered. The Helicarrier was filthy. She couldn't let it stay that way.

"Let's scrub these floors and clean our desks, equipment, and boots before the Avengers return," she said.

The crew jumped into action, preparing to follow each of Maria's orders.

Across the bridge, Director Nick Fury monitored the Avengers. They were responding to a bizarre threat in South America: several dinosaurs had appeared out of thin air and begun eating everything in sight!

Nick watched as Hulk threw a punch at a *T. rex*. Iron Man flew around the vicious creature, trying to distract it. The *T. rex* snapped its jaws, narrowly missing Captain America.

Nick sat back, enjoying the show. The dinosaurs didn't stand a chance against Earth's Mightiest Heroes.

"Never a dull moment with them," Fury said as Thor flew into view.

"You can say that again!" Maria said. "Which is why we need to get things done as quickly as possible. Who *knows* when the next disaster is going to strike!"

Agent Hill smiled as the crew tightened bolts on machines, emptied desk drawers, and even did the dishes!

"I love it when a plan comes together!" she exclaimed.

"I wouldn't call this a victory just yet," Fury remarked from a weather console. "Instruments show that the Helicarrier is headed into some kind of storm front like nothing we've ever seen before."

Just then, purple and green lightning flashed through the windows.

"What kind of lightning bolts are those?" Maria asked.

"The kind that follow the thunderclaps of history's mightiest time storm!" a voice boomed. It was Kang.

"The future belongs to Kang," the conqueror explained, appearing on the bridge. "And now so shall the past!"

Turning, Kang fired a blast at a nearby crew member. To Maria's amazement, Kang's blasts didn't destroy the people and objects they hit—they *aged* them! Steel consoles rusted, and glass warped and cracked.

"With the Avengers away, no one can stop me from aging S.H.I.E.L.D. to dust," the villain explained. "And then the past will belong to Kang the Conqueror, just like the future!"

"The dinosaurs in South America—you brought them here to keep the Avengers busy?" Nick Fury asked.

"Of course," Kang said, cackling. "All of time—past, present, and future—is at my disposal."

Fury threw a switch, and a force field lowered over Kang.

"Didn't see *that* coming, did you?" Fury laughed.

"You fools," Kang cried. "Do you really believe your puny tricks can stop me? I am a time traveler! I will call on a future self to free me!"

At that moment, another Kang appeared. Hitting a button, he freed the trapped Kang.

Nick Fury turned to Maria Hill. "This is starting to give me a headache," he said.

"No kidding," a heroic voice shouted from above.

Both Kangs spun around to see the mighty Avengers!

The Avengers had tamed the dinosaurs! Now, the powerful beasts fought *with* them.

Hulk's *Tyrannosaurus rex* gave a rumbling roar as the heroes surrounded the time-traveling villains.

"What doth thine reptilian beast say?" Thor asked Hulk.

Hulk smiled.

"*T. rex* say 'SMASH!'"

"You heard him!" Iron Man called.

With that, the Avengers—and their dinosaurs—charged toward the Kangs.

The Kangs had seen enough of history to realize they were hopelessly outmatched by the collective power of Earth's Mightiest Heroes.

"Until next time, heroes!" Kang called out as he and his older self leaped forward into the future.

As the dust settled and things returned to normal, Iron Man turned to Captain America. "This place is a wreck," he said.

"Iron Man's right, Agent Hill," Cap began. "When is S.H.I.E.L.D. going to start cleaning up around here?"

Maria Hill sighed as Nick Fury gave her a wink with his good eye. "No time like the present," he said.

Call for Backup

Billionaire inventor Tony Stark loved new technology. His company, Stark Industries, had been hard at work on a new spaceship that could safely take groups of tourists to the moon. Finally, it was ready for its first flight.

Putting on his Iron Man armor, Tony flew alongside the ship as it blasted off.

A short time later, Iron Man greeted the ship's passengers at the new Stark Industries Moon Base. Iron Man had invited very important people, including leaders in government and business from all around the world, to be part of the first group to visit the base.

Suddenly, the tourists' fun was interrupted by a huge crash!

"Don't worry," Iron Man assured the group. "It's probably nothing dangerous. I'll go check it out."

But secretly, Iron Man was worried. *What could have caused that crash?* he wondered as he rocketed toward the crash site.

Iron Man called his teammates, the Avengers, to help.

"We're in the middle of a battle with Hydra," said Captain America over the communicator. "We'll get there as soon as we can, but it could take some time."

For now, Iron Man was on his own!

Iron Man was right to be worried. Emerging from the crash site was Thanos, an evil ruler from deep space who wanted nothing more than to take over Earth!

And Thanos wasn't alone. He had brought along his army of Outriders—a race of alien warriors, each with four strong arms, long claws, and razor-sharp teeth!

Iron Man was in serious trouble. With the Avengers occupied, he called the only other group that might be able to help!

Deep in space, on the bridge of their mighty starship, the Guardians of the Galaxy received Iron Man's distress call.

"Tony Stark's in trouble," reported Star-Lord, the brave leader of the Guardians.

"Let's go," said Drax, a fierce alien soldier.

"How can we get there in time?" asked the green-skinned Gamora. "We're halfway across the galaxy!"

"I am Groot," remarked the plant creature, Groot.

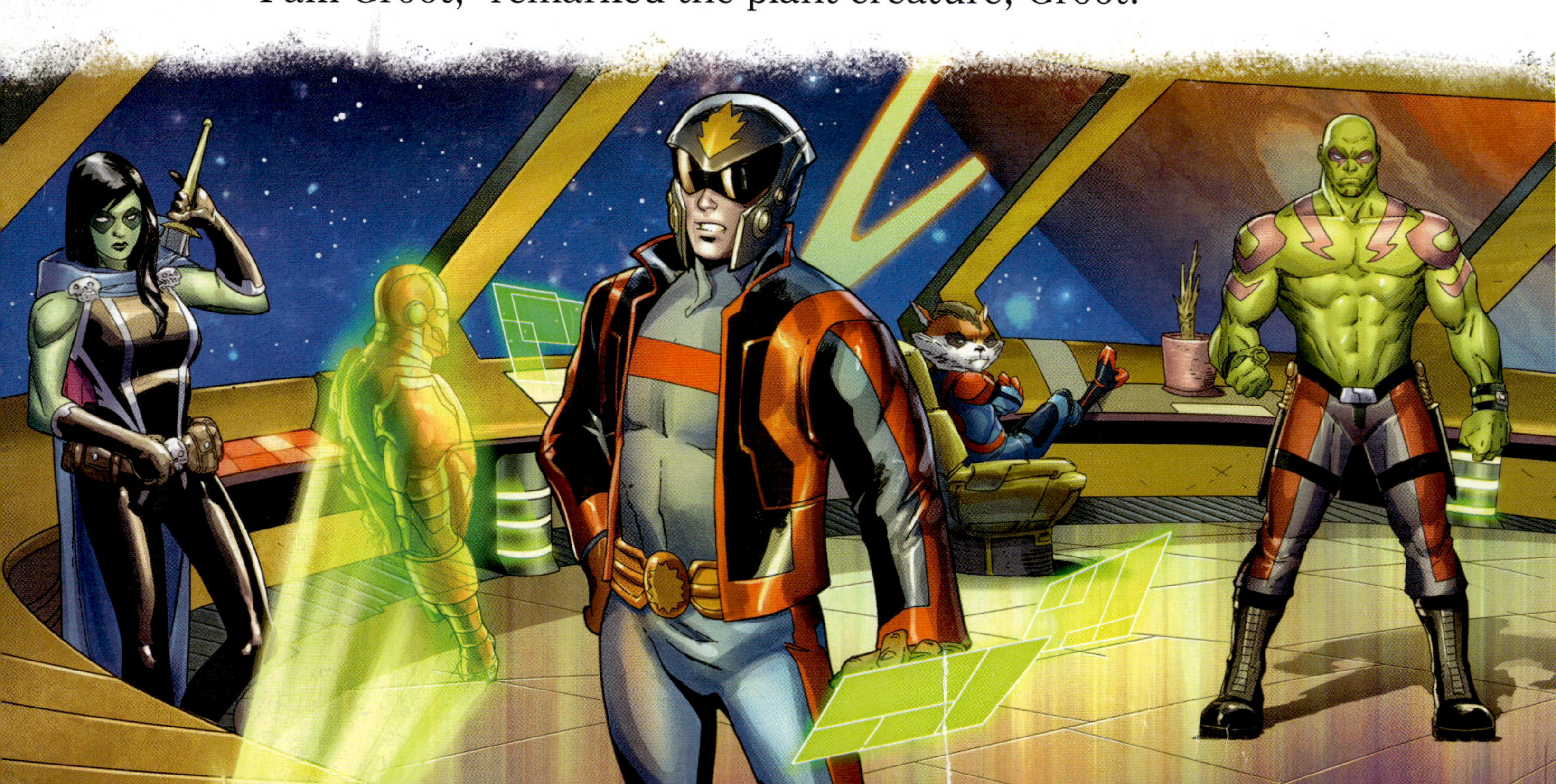

"Good point, Groot," said Rocket Raccoon, a small but skilled mercenary. Groot only ever said "I am Groot," but Rocket always knew what he meant. "Groot thinks we should ask the Nova Corps for a boost."

Star-Lord radioed the Nova Corps, a group of interstellar peacekeepers. "We need an emergency teleport to Earth's moon," he said.

Happy to help, the Novas quickly initiated a teleportation beam that sent the Guardians through space!

As soon as the Guardians arrived, they jumped into battle!

"What took you so long?" complained Iron Man, who had been forced to the ground by the Outriders.

"We come all the way from the other side of the galaxy, and this is the thanks we get?" asked Rocket.

"I am Groot," added Groot.

"Time for battle!" yelled Gamora, smashing the Outriders.

"Guardians, don't hold back on these guys!" ordered Star-Lord.

Forced to fight the Guardians, the Outriders backed off Iron Man. The armored Avenger was able to pick himself up and defend himself against his attackers.

"You sure know how to get into trouble, Stark," joked Rocket.

While the Guardians and Iron Man were fighting the Outriders, Thanos headed toward the moon base.

That's when Iron Man understood Thanos's plan. "He must be trying to capture everyone at the base," Iron Man said. "So many of Earth's important leaders are there. Thanos could grab them all at once!"

Without its greatest leaders, the planet would be weaker. Thanos could invade and proclaim himself ruler!

But Thanos didn't get far. At that moment, the mighty Avengers arrived in their Quinjet.

"Avengers, assemble!" shouted Captain America, directing the team in combat.

"That's right. If you want a shot at Earth, you'll have to go through us first," Hawkeye announced.

"Hulk smash!" yelled the battle-ready Hulk, racing toward Thanos.

The Avengers combined their powers and abilities in an attempt to stop Thanos.

"Have at thee, villain!" Thor shouted, hurling his mighty hammer.

"That goes for all of us," Falcon agreed as he swooped in.

"We will stop you, Thanos," promised Black Widow.

But despite the team's best efforts, Thanos was still gaining ground.

Iron Man scanned Thanos and discovered something new. "That device at his belt—he's never had that before," he said. "Could that machine be what helped Thanos travel here?"

Thanos had arrived on the moon in a big crash. But Iron Man didn't see a ship anywhere, and Thanos was unharmed. He must have used some kind of new technology!

Quickly, Iron Man formed a plan. He needed Groot. The little plant creature held some big secrets.

"I'm going to need your special talents here, buddy," Iron Man said to Groot.

"I am Groot," replied Groot.

"You bet you are!" agreed Iron Man.

Iron Man flew Groot over Thanos and dropped him right into the middle of the fight.

"Bombs away!" the armored Avenger shouted.

As he fell, Groot transformed from a little plant into a giant plant!

"What is this?" said the surprised Thanos as Groot seemed to appear out of nowhere.

"I am Groot," Groot yelled, delivering blow after crushing blow to Thanos.

Thanos was so distracted by Groot's sudden attack that he didn't notice Iron Man swoop in and steal the device from his belt!

Studying the device, Iron Man figured out how to reverse its effects. He pressed a button and a sphere of energy formed around Thanos and the Outriders!

With another push of a button, Iron Man sent the villains shooting away from the surface of the moon.

"Nooooo!" Thanos screamed as he flew away.

"Where are you sending them, Tony?" asked Captain America.

"Back to where they came from," responded Iron Man. "Without this device, we won't see them back here anytime soon!"

Back on the moon base, Earth's leaders and their families were happy to be safe from Thanos and eager to meet their heroes! Thanks to the Avengers and their friends the Guardians of the Galaxy, the trip to the moon was a great success!

Hail, Hydra!

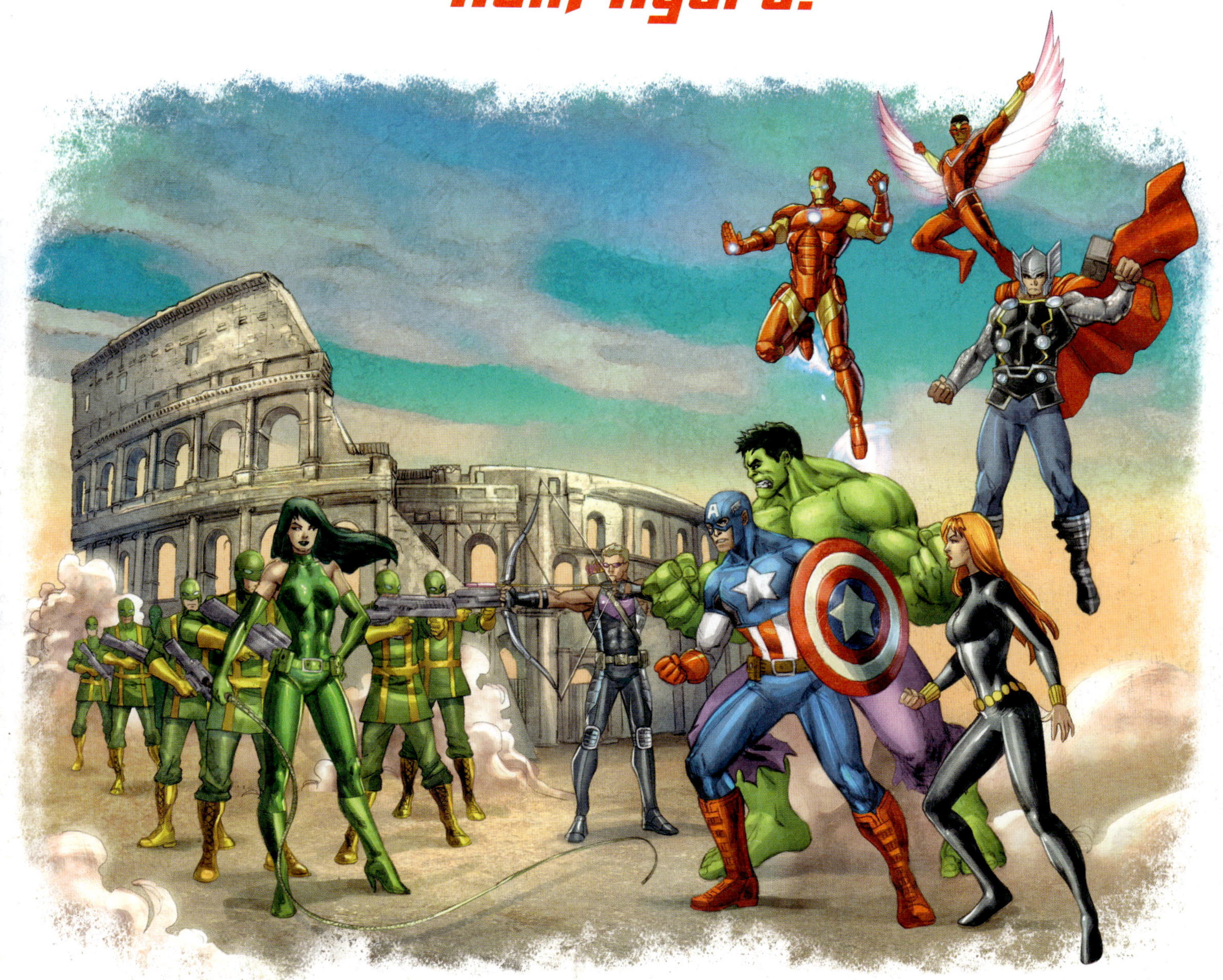

"Arrivederci!" Black Widow shouted as she blocked a jab from the evil Madame Hydra. The Avenger had been chasing the Super Villain all over Europe. She had finally tracked Madame Hydra and her agents to the Colosseum in Rome.

"Charming. You speak Italian," Madame Hydra replied. Then, using her enhanced strength, Madame Hydra lifted some debris from the Colosseum and threw it at the heroine with all her might.

Nearby, tourists looked on in shock and awe.

As the fight continued, it became clear that Black Widow would not be able to stop Madame Hydra alone. She was beginning to weaken. How much longer could she continue this battle?

Suddenly, a repulsor beam blasted at the ground. Iron Man swooped in, knocking Madame Hydra backward. Meanwhile, Captain America and Hulk ran toward Black Widow.

When the smoke cleared, Madame Hydra was gone.

"She has the Mayday computer virus," Black Widow said. "Her cyber attack could crash all the computers in Europe."

"Don't worry. She won't get far," Iron Man said. "We have a homing device on her. She's going to lead us right to her lair."

"We'll meet the rest of the team there," Cap said. "Avengers, assemble!"

The Avengers followed the homing beacon to Madame Hydra's top-secret villa in the Italian countryside. They had hoped to surprise her, but she was waiting for them—with a giant Hydra tank!

"Go on!" Thor told his friends. "I will handle this."

Thor spun his mighty hammer and launched it at the tank, but it barely made a dent. The tank turned its turret and fired! The force of the blast knocked Thor through the sky.

"By Odin, this metal beast is stronger than it looks," Thor said.

Meanwhile, Iron Man took the direct approach and blasted open the door to the villa. Captain America and Black Widow quickly followed his lead as several Hydra agents attacked.

As Hulk entered the villa, two agents dropped a large electrified metal cage from the ceiling, instantly trapping him!

Hawkeye tried to unlock the cage, but his attempts only seemed to make the cage stronger. Then he noticed a sniper agent in an alcove. He quickly shot an arrow to stop him.

"Greetings, Avengers," Madame Hydra cackled as Hydra agents gathered behind her.

"I don't want to fight you," Iron Man said as he hovered above her. "But since you made such an entrance, I'll make an exception."

Madame Hydra grabbed a whip from one of her men and lashed out at Iron Man's armor. "You'll have to do better than that," the armored Avenger said.

"I intend to," the Super Villain replied before yelling, "Hail, Hydra!"

At the sound of her scream, the entire Hydra army came out of hiding. They attacked with all their might, swinging swords, firing beams from high-tech ray guns, and throwing nets, all with furious anger and grim determination.

Meanwhile, outside Madame Hydra's villa, Thor was still battling the massive Hydra tank. Hearing the battle cries from inside the villa, Thor gripped his hammer more tightly and furrowed his brow, intent on stopping the tank once and for all.

The tank fired another blast, and Thor jumped away with only seconds to spare. The Asgardian raised Mjolnir high above his head and brought it down with a thunderous crash. As the hammer hit the ground, a bolt of lightning streaked down from the heavens and hit the tank, electrifying it and shorting it out. A victorious Thor stood before the defeated, demolished, smoking tank, dissatisfied with having had to use lightning to stop the technological terror. Perhaps he would find glorious battle inside the villa.

Thor crashed through a window into the villa only to see a caged Hulk. As he lifted his hammer to break the restraints, he heard someone call, "Wait—don't touch the cage! It multiplies any impact." It was Hawkeye. He was still trying to free the green Goliath and turn the tide of the battle. "You hit that with Mjolnir, you'll be knocked back to Asgard."

Thor nodded. He knew what to do. "Hang on to something," he instructed Hawkeye. "It is about to get very windy."

Thor spun Mjolnir around and around. The winds picked up. Then they picked up some more. Hydra agents were thrown about by the gusts. A small cyclone formed around the cage, lifting it—and Hulk—right off the ground! Seconds later, Hulk—and the Hydra agents—fell to the ground with a *THUD*!

"Right," said Hawkeye. "That's one way to do it. Now let's find and stop Madame Hydra!" And with that, the three heroes raced off to join the others.

With the rest of the Avengers joining the fight, Madame Hydra knew she and her Hydra army were outmatched. She had to activate the Mayday virus immediately!

Madame Hydra raced to the underground control room, but Iron Man was hot on her heels. The armored Avenger fired a blast at the wall behind her. It exploded, revealing the secret control room.

"Not another step, heroes!" Madame Hydra yelled, walking up to the control panel. "Or else I release the virus!"

Just then, an electric blast hit Madame Hydra in the side. It had come from Black Widow! With her gauntlet still smoking from firing the blast, the heroine leaped at the villain and knocked her to the ground!

As the Avengers gathered around them, Black Widow smiled at the defeated villain. "Where were we? Oh, yes, I remember—Arrivederci, madame, or shall I say 'ciao'?"

Black Widow laughed and then radioed their location to Nick Fury.

As S.H.I.E.L.D. agents stormed the villa and took Madame Hydra and her agents away, Iron Man called down the Quinjet.

"Time to go home, gang," Iron Man said, raising his faceplate to reveal billionaire inventor Tony Stark beneath.

"Not so fast," Black Widow said. "I didn't track Madame Hydra to Italy to leave without dinner. Anyone up for some fine Italian food? Tony's buying," she said with a smile.

"When in Rome," said Tony, "do as the Romans do. *Mangia*!"

Attack of Count Nefaria

The Avengers were returning from a dangerous mission in Italy when they received an urgent message from S.H.I.E.L.D. Director Nick Fury.

"Avengers, priceless paintings and rare sculptures have been stolen from museums in and around New York City," Fury said. "Just this morning, someone took an ancient Egyptian amulet that is rumored to have supernatural powers. S.H.I.E.L.D. believes the man responsible for the theft is—"

"Count Nefaria," interrupted billionaire Tony Stark—who was also the hero Iron Man. "He's been stealing art all over the world. He uses it as cash in his criminal underworld."

"Perfect timing," Captain America remarked as the Quinjet landed on the roof of the Stark Industries building in the heart of bustling New York City. "We'll look into it!"

Iron Man quickly scanned New York's emergency frequencies. An alarm had just gone off at the Metropolitan Museum of Art. The Avengers knew they had to investigate!

"You go to the museum," Captain America told the other Avengers. "I have another idea. I'll catch up with you as soon as I can."

Thor and Iron Man flew toward the museum. The other Avengers followed close behind, hopping over cabs and cars as they weaved their way through New York City's traffic-filled streets.

Dr. Bruce Banner knew the team would need his help. As they ran down New York's Fifth Avenue, he let loose his inner anger, releasing Hulk.

"Don't destroy the city, Hulk!" Iron Man shouted to the green giant. "We haven't even found our villain yet!"

Inside the museum, the Avengers tracked the sound of the alarm. It was coming from the Temple of Dendur exhibit.

"I wonder what someone would want from *here*," Black Widow said, eyeing the massive Egyptian ruins as they crept through the exhibit.

Just then, the Avengers spotted a mysterious cloaked figure skulking through the temple.

"Gotcha!" Iron Man called. He was about to shoot a repulsor beam when he noticed that the thief was standing in front of a priceless artifact.

"Would you mind?" he asked Black Widow. "I don't want to damage the exhibit."

"My pleasure," Black Widow said. With a few flips, she landed in front of the thief. But the crook refused to talk.

Across the room, the incredible Hulk lumbered toward the thief. He knew just what to do.

Hulk lifted the thug high in the air and let out a mighty roar. "Hulk smash puny human!" he yelled.

The crook could handle a lot, but Hulk scared him. He reluctantly admitted to working with Count Nefaria.

"I'm supposed to meet him at a secret art auction across town. . . . I'll give you the exact location!" he cried.

"Now was that so hard?" Black Widow asked with a sly smile.

The Avengers radioed Captain America, who met them outside an old warehouse on the west side. Looking through a window, they saw thugs, goons, and mobsters.

"When this auction is over, Count Nefaria will have enough money to rule the criminal underworld," Hawkeye said.

"Then we need to stop him—" Captain America started.

"Hulk will!" Hulk roared as he burst through the wall.

Hulk grabbed two of the mobsters.

"Where's the count?" Cap yelled at them, but they wouldn't talk.

Suddenly, a group of the count's men attacked!

Thor threw his hammer, knocking down the crooks like bowling pins. As one of the mobsters aimed a blaster at a piece of art, Cap raised his shield. The Avengers had to be careful: they would need to return all the art unharmed!

With the other Avengers locked in battle, Black Widow and Hawkeye searched for Count Nefaria.

"I see him!" Hawkeye called out. He aimed his arrow at the Super Villain and fired, catching the count by his cape.

"You hung the count like one of his stolen art pieces!" Black Widow joked.

"Except it's a bit crooked," Hawkeye said.

Elsewhere in the warehouse, the other Avengers defeated Count Nefaria's men.

"This is one art auction where I am leaving empty-handed and happy about it," Iron Man said when the Avengers joined Black Widow and Hawkeye.

"You found me," Count Nefaria said, "but can you stop me?"

Count Nefaria pulled an Egyptian amulet out of his pocket. He whispered an ancient spell, and the amulet began to glow.

Suddenly, a beam shot out of the amulet and a giant two-headed snake materialized in the middle of the room. It wrapped its scaly body around the Avengers and bared its fangs. The Avengers were defenseless against the mighty beast!

Mustering all his strength, Hulk broke himself free from the snake's grasp. Then, with a mighty punch, he knocked the fangs out of one of its mouths.

Thor turned to Hulk and spun his hammer. "Well done, Hulk," the Asgardian said. "Now, snake, have at thee!"

As Hulk fought the super snake, Thor worked to free the other Avengers.

Hawkeye and Black Widow faced off against the count, but he blocked all their attacks! Then Cap threw his shield, knocking Count Nefaria off his feet.

Suddenly, a large shadow fell across the count. It was the snake's! Hulk had thrown the beast at the count and it trapped him.

The Avengers cheered for the incredible Hulk. He'd saved his friends and defeated Count Nefaria!

S.H.I.E.L.D. took Count Nefaria and the rest of the criminals into custody, and the Avengers took the Egyptian amulet back to the Metropolitan Museum of Art.

"Back in its proper place for the world to see," Black Widow remarked.

"And so are the paintings. Thanks to Hulk, New York City's art world has been restored," Cap said.

Hulk smiled. It felt good to save the day!

Play Ball!

"This is so weird," said Iron Man.

"Says the guy who's fought off alien invasions?" replied Black Widow.

The Avengers were playing a charity baseball expo in Manhattan's Central Park.

Captain America stepped up to the plate and pointed to the outfield, indicating that he was about to hit a homer.

"Surely you jest," Thor said from the pitcher's mound.

"I am the Asgardian prince of thunder," Thor continued. "Lightning is mine to command. And you, my friend, are a mere mortal."

"Yup," Captain America said, grinning. "But you're still not going to be able to get that ball past me."

"See? I told you baseball was dumb," said Iron Man. "Now it's even caused Cap to lose his mind."

Thor threw the baseball so fast that he caused a sonic boom. The rest of the Avengers couldn't even *see* the ball!

Captain America swung the bat.

A quarter of a second later, there was a loud *CRACK*, and the ball flew over a mile away. Captain America smiled.

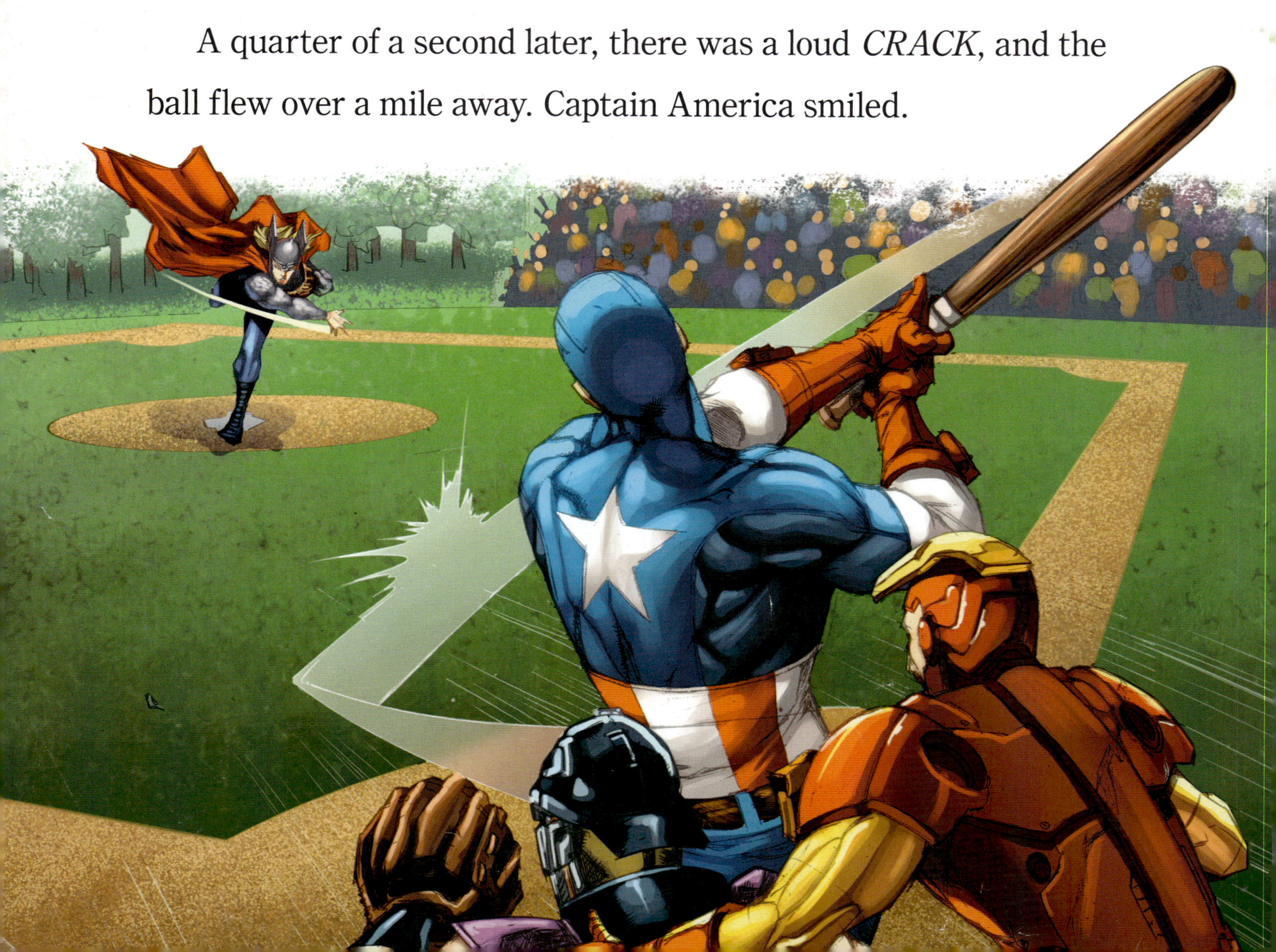

“I got it!” yelled Falcon as he took off into the sky to catch the ball.

“But . . . but . . .” said Thor, utterly surprised that Cap had been able to get a hit off him.

“Hulk want turn,” Hulk said, stomping his foot.

Hulk took the bat and stepped up to home plate. The green giant stomped his foot again. He had been waiting patiently for a turn at bat, but he was done waiting. He was ready for his turn!

Just then, the ground began to shake, but it wasn't from the incredible Hulk.

"Hey . . ." Black Widow said, looking around. "You feel that?"

The ground exploded! Rocks flew everywhere and thick smoke filled the air.

The formerly calm Central Park erupted in chaos. The crowd that had gathered for a fun Sunday afternoon game began to scream and run in terror, knocking each other over in their hurry to get to safety.

The Avengers looked around. They were usually ready for anything, but they hadn't expected *this*. What was going on?

Finally, the ground stopped quaking and the smoke began to clear. A sinister figure slowly emerged from the cracked and broken earth.

Black Widow narrowed her eyes. She knew this villain. "Tyrannus," she said.

Tyrannus was a dangerous, immortal scientist who had long ago taken a drink from the fountain of youth.

The Avengers had faced Tyrannus before, but he had always managed to get away. The Super Villain's science was so advanced it seemed like magic. Even Bruce Banner's incredible mind could not rival him.

Tyrannus had ruled the underworld since the Roman Empire. He had an army of minions at his disposal. But the evil scientist wanted more. He wanted to rule the overworld, as well. And he was there to take what he wanted!

Tyrannus rose out of the smoking pit in the ground, brilliant blue energy sparkling and crackling from his powerful sword.

"Pathetic," the Super Villain sneered, looking down at the Avengers in disgust. "Wasting your time with silly human games. I knew you'd be too distracted to sense me coming." The villain laughed. "At last I will defeat the mighty Avengers and take over the world you are so fond of!"

"Avengers!" Captain America called. "Those people need help!"

"We're on it!" yelled Black Widow as the Avengers rushed into action. They had to get the innocent civilians to safety—and fast.

"Not you two," Tyrannus said to Thor and Hulk. "I have something else in mind for you."

One of Tyrannus's powers was mind control. He used it to cause Thor and Hulk to see each other as enemies.

The befuddled behemoths began to battle.

Hulk clobbered Thor with his fists. Then Thor struck Hulk with his hammer, throwing the green giant backward. Regaining his balance, Hulk thundered toward Thor.

"If we can't stop Hulk and Thor from fighting, they'll destroy New York City," Captain America yelled. "Iron Man!"

"On it," Iron Man said calmly, firing a blast at Tyrannus.

Meanwhile, Cap threw his shield toward the fighting friends.

Thor and Hulk reached out to hit each other just as Cap's shield passed between them.

KA-BOOM!

The heroes' fists collided with Cap's unbreakable shield and caused a giant shock wave. The blast was so strong that it knocked Tyrannus—and the heroes—clear across the baseball diamond.

Slowly, Hulk and Thor awoke from their trance. The two heroes looked around.

"What happened?" Thor asked.

"You guys went boom. It was awful . . . even worse than baseball, if you can believe that," Iron Man said. "Now, let's see if Black Widow and Falcon need any help."

An hour later, S.H.I.E.L.D. had cleaned up the park and taken Tyrannus away. It was time to finish the game.

"Hulk hit ball now?" Hulk asked.

Iron Man shrugged and looked up at the sky. "I'm not sure Falcon can fly all the way to the moon, but sure, why not? Batter up!"

Thor Versus the Avengers

It was a bright, sunny day in New York City. Captain America and Black Widow were patrolling when they received an urgent call from S.H.I.E.L.D. about a disturbance downtown.

Cap and Black Widow raced to the scene. They arrived to find an entire army of charging Asgardians. Leading them was Thor!

"There must be a big problem for Thor to think we need all these Asgardians," Captain America said to Black Widow.

Black Widow looked around. "I don't know. This feels strange, Captain," she said.

Just then, they heard a nearby man cry out, "Help! Captain America! The aliens are going to attack us!"

Cap realized that Thor and the Asgardians *were* the disturbance S.H.I.E.L.D. had called him about! "Thor," Captain America yelled. "What's going on?"

Thor didn't answer. Instead, he signaled the Asgardians to intensify their attack!

Captain America and Black Widow realized they had no choice but to defend the people of Earth against the Asgardian army. Captain America used his shield to knock a sword out of an enemy warrior's hand. Before it hit the ground, Black Widow caught the sword and used its hilt to knock out another Asgardian.

"We need help!" Black Widow yelled as she signaled to Hawkeye, who had just arrived with Hulk.

But Hawkeye wasn't paying attention to her. He and the incredible Hulk had followed a different army of Asgardians into an abandoned warehouse.

"Smash!" Hulk yelled.

"Shhh, Hulk. We're trying to sneak up on them!" Hawkeye said. "What's wrong with them? I wish Thor were here."

Suddenly, Hawkeye heard a noise behind him and spun around, drawing an arrow out of his quiver. It was Thor!

“Thor? I almost shot you!” Hawkeye said.

“Smash!” Hulk shouted, running toward Thor.

“Hulk, what are you doing? That’s our friend!” Hawkeye said. But Thor still wasn’t saying anything. “Thor . . . ?”

Hulk charged Thor, but the Asgardian was just an illusion and the green Goliath hit a thick support beam. As the pillar crumbled, the walls shook and the ceiling cracked. Soon the building was falling down around them!

Meanwhile, high up in the air, Iron Man and Falcon saw the building begin to crumble. They flew over as fast as they could. "Quick, we have to get in there and help them!" Falcon said.

"Already on it," Iron Man said, zooming past Falcon. The pair reached the building just in time to pull Hawkeye out of the wreckage. Luckily, Hulk had managed to hold up enough of the building to keep his teammate safe.

"It was . . . it was Thor!"

But it *wasn't* Thor. At least, not the *real* Thor. The Asgardian had heard the sirens, too, and flew downtown to see what was happening.

When Thor arrived, he was shocked to see an entire troop of Asgardians attacking a bridge full of trapped civilians.

"Brothers, what are you doing here?" Thor asked, landing on the bridge. Instead of answering, the Asgardians raised their swords.

“Run!” Thor told the civilians, but they seemed just as afraid of him as they were of the Asgardians. What was going on? Why were the Asgardians attacking, and why were the civilians so frightened of Thor? He had to give the civilians time to get away, but Thor didn’t want to hurt his own people!

Before the Asgardians could reach Thor, he slammed Mjolnir against the bridge. The shock wave knocked out the warriors.

Thor knew something was wrong. He needed the Avengers.

Suddenly, Thor heard more shouts coming from beneath him. A group of civilians were pointing at the sky.

Thor raised Mjolnir and turned to see . . . himself?

Now Thor *really* knew something strange was happening. How could there be two of him?

"What is this trickery?" Thor asked.

The other Thor just smiled.

Thor realized it was time he got to the bottom of this mystery. With a great cry, he called down a huge lightning bolt. The sky grew dark and crackled with energy. Thor pointed his hammer at his foe.

The bolt of lightning hit the other Thor, who disappeared!

Thor heard a slow clap and a low laugh behind him. He turned around to find the villain smiling at him. It was his mischievous brother, Loki.

"Brother, it has been a long time," Thor said.

"Not long enough," Loki replied.

"What are you doing?" Thor asked.

"I'm robbing Earth of one of its so-called heroes!" Loki answered. "When this world sees you and your Asgardian army attacking innocent civilians, they will never trust you again. You'll be an exile, just as you have forced me to be."

Thor realized that the other Thor must have been one of Loki's mirages. He couldn't believe his brother would go to such lengths to hurt him. He needed to turn the Asgardian army to his side.

"I have all the Asgardians under my control," Loki said, as if reading Thor's mind. "They won't help you!"

"The Avengers . . ." Thor began.

"They won't help you, either. With my Thor mirages, I've made sure they'll never trust you again!" Loki said with a laugh.

"You underestimate us, Brother. The Avengers trust each other. We will not be broken up by one of your tricks!" Thor said.

"What a fool you are," Loki laughed. "Where are your friends now?"

"Right behind you," Iron Man said.

Loki turned around, shocked! Iron Man, Captain America, Hulk, Black Widow, Hawkeye, and Falcon were all right behind him.

"But . . . but," Loki stammered, for once at a loss for words.

"You will not win this day, Loki. Surrender, and let us end this," Thor said.

"How is this possible?" Loki asked the Avengers.

"I trust my friends," Thor said.

"And we trust you, buddy," Captain America said. "We knew as soon as Fake Thor began attacking us that there had to be some sort of explanation!"

But Loki was not one to give up. With a sneer, he raised his staff, and the army of Asgardians began to attack!

While the rest of the Avengers fought to knock out the Asgardians, Thor ran toward Loki. He knew that his brother's staff must be what was keeping his people under Loki's command. If he could break it, the Asgardians would be free once more.

Thor summoned a bolt of lightning, but Loki deflected the bolt. It hit Thor and threw him back against a nearby building.

The mighty Mjolnir flew out of Thor's hands and Thor slumped to the ground.

"I've defeated you again, Brother," Loki said. "The Asgardians will continue to attack, and there is no way to stop them." He turned to walk away.

"Never," Thor said. Thor raised his hand and summoned Mjolnir. As the mighty hammer flew toward Thor, it smashed into Loki's staff, breaking it in two!

Suddenly, the Asgardians stopped fighting. With Loki's staff broken, they were now free of his control. The warriors surrounded Loki. He could not escape!

"I'll return, Thor," Loki said as the Asgardians took him away.

The Avengers assembled around Thor. As people cheered, Thor smiled. Thor was a hero again and the Avengers were once more a team. Together, they would continue to fight to protect the world!

Double Take

Being a member of the mighty Avengers is a big challenge—especially for Avengers like Hawkeye, Black Widow, and Falcon. Unlike their teammates, their skills come mainly from their training and their equipment, not from special powers.

So even on a beautiful day in Manhattan, it was no surprise to find these three heroes sharpening their skills in a special gymnasium inside Avengers Tower. While Hawkeye practiced his target shooting and Black Widow ran an obstacle course to test her speed and agility, Falcon flew complicated aerial patterns.

But training ended when a video call came in from the invincible Iron Man!

"Sorry to interrupt, Avengers, but I have a mission for you."

Iron Man explained that S.H.I.E.L.D. had found a handheld device that could open a hole to another dimension—specifically, the Negative Zone!

"The Negative Zone!" Black Widow interrupted. "That's where we imprison criminals too dangerous to go to normal jails!"

Among the worst of the criminals imprisoned in the Negative Zone was a group of evil Skrulls, who could change shape to look like anyone they chose.

Iron Man nodded. "That's right, Black Widow. The device is too dangerous to be left in anyone else's hands, so S.H.I.E.L.D. is giving it to the Avengers for safekeeping. A special courier is bringing it by train to New York in an hour. I need you three to meet him at the station."

Hawkeye and Black Widow put on coats over their costumes so they wouldn't be recognized on the busy New York streets.

"We don't have much time to get to the train station," Falcon pointed out. "I'll fly ahead and meet you two there."

Falcon took to the skies with his pet bird, Redwing. Suddenly, a figure flew at him. Falcon was ready for almost anything, but he wasn't expecting to be attacked by . . . himself!

It didn't take Falcon long to figure out what was happening. *Another Falcon?* he thought. *It must be a Skrull!*

"I bet you want to take my place and get that device so you can free your friends from the Negative Zone!" shouted Falcon. "But that's not going to happen!"

"We'll see," said Falcon's Skrull double. "Even if you manage to stop me, we still have doubles of your friends Black Widow and Hawkeye."

Falcon tried to radio his friends to warn them, but all he heard was static. *The Skrull must be jamming my signal*, he thought. Now what was he going to do?

Knowing it was more important than ever that he get to the station first, Falcon hurled himself at the high-flying Skrull! But the Skrull and the real Falcon were so perfectly matched that even Redwing couldn't tell which one was which!

Meanwhile, on a crowded subway, the disguised Hawkeye and Black Widow noticed a couple of shadowy figures—a man and a woman—staring at them from the corner of the train car.

The Avengers moved in to get a closer look at the couple. Realizing they'd been noticed, the figures leaped to their feet, revealing themselves to be identical doubles for Hawkeye and Black Widow!

"Skrulls!" shouted Black Widow, removing her coat and firing an energy blast from her bracelet.

"Watch out for the other passengers!" Hawkeye warned, opening his coat and pulling out his bow.

But the Skrulls weren't as careful. They didn't care *who* they hit.

The train stopped and the passengers fled. By the time the doors closed, only the Avengers and the Skrulls were still aboard.

The two pairs faced each other down, weapons drawn. A few moments later, the subway pulled into Grand Central Terminal.

Both Hawkeyes and both Black Widows charged through the station and arrived at the S.H.I.E.L.D. train platform, where they found two Falcons waiting.

The S.H.I.E.L.D. train door opened and the mysterious courier came out.

It was Captain America!

Cap looked carefully at the two groups of Avengers, trying to figure out which ones were really his friends.

Holding the dimension-warping device in his strong gloved hand, he addressed the group: "Glad to see some of you. Anyone want to tell me which of you are the real Avengers and which will be taking a trip to the Negative Zone?"

One of the Hawkeyes spoke up first. "They're the Skrulls, Cap—they came after us because we don't have powers, so we're the weakest members of the team!"

Hearing that, Captain America turned the device on one of the teams. As they disappeared, they regained their true forms.

"Nice work, Cap," the real Falcon said gratefully. "But how could you be so sure they were the Skrulls?"

"They may have looked just like you," Captain America explained, "but the Skrulls made one big mistake."

"What was that?" asked Hawkeye.

"No Avenger would ever say it was their powers that made them strong. Once your double said that, I knew who was who."

And with that, the Avengers returned to Avengers Tower to resume their training, because it was their hard work and dedication that made them Earth's Mightiest Heroes.

Jurassic Central Park

It had been a long week for the mighty Avengers. First they had taken on Thanos. Then they had battled Kang and Count Nefaria. Now it was time to rest!

Dr. Bruce Banner and billionaire inventor Tony Stark were enjoying a lazy day in Tony's lab, where Tony kept all his cool gadgets and inventions.

"So . . . wanna build something?" Tony asked Bruce.

Bruce shrugged. "Sure. But something small."

Three hours later, Nick Fury burst into Tony's lab. "Stark!" he yelled. "What did you do?"

Fury pointed at a massive portal that was opening in Central Park.

Tony cringed. "We may have built a teeny, tiny . . . time machine."

"You built a time machine?" Fury yelled. "To what period?"

Before Tony could answer, something big came through the portal. Several somethings, in fact.

Terrifying tyrannosaurs, velociraptors with razor-sharp teeth, and pterodactyls with winged claws rushed through, roaring at everything in their way! The time machine had opened a portal to the Jurassic period!

"I'm not one to tattle," Tony said, "but Bruce helped."

Fury leaned in. "Then I would get him mad . . . and quick!"

Tony stepped into his Iron Man armor and rocketed toward the menacing carnivores. But he wasn't alone. The incredible Hulk was right behind him!

"I wish Falcon were here," Iron Man said, firing a repulsor beam at an incoming pterodactyl. "Maybe he speaks their language."

"Hulk speak language!" the green Goliath said as he rammed into a *Tyrannosaurus Rex*. "Hulk ROAR!!!!!"

As more and more dinosaurs came through the portal, the battle quickly turned disastrous.

Hulk tried to stay on top, but he was overpowered by a group of dinosaurs!

Iron Man struggled with a raptor that was crushing his armor with its mighty jaw!

"Ya know," Iron Man cried as he tried to avoid a series of razor-sharp claws, "this . . . isn't . . . going as planned!"

"Remind me to never, *ever* play with Pym's particle beam again!" Iron Man said. "I knew crossing those wires would create a portal to another time . . . but I was hoping for the seventies!"

Just as the *T. rex* and the pterodactyl were about to take giant chomps out of the Super Heroes, a powerful force whizzed by Hulk, pushing him to the ground. It rocked the *T. rex*, sending it flying across the park.

"What was—" Iron Man began, but before he could finish, something flew past him, too. A loud explosion knocked a pterodactyl out of the sky and a blast sent the *T. rex* tumbling to the ground.

Hulk gathered himself off the floor and smiled.

"'Bout time you showed up!" Iron Man said with a smile.

It was the other mighty Avengers!

Iron Man shook Captain America's hand. "Hey, Cap," he said. "Let me guess. Fury told you about our tiny issue with a couple of lizards?"

"Tiny?" Cap repeated, looking up at a roaring *T. rex*.

Thor stepped forward. "Let's even the score. What say you?"

Hulk grinned. "I SAY YOU!"

The Avengers launched themselves into the fray. With a few repulsor blasts from Iron Man, some trick shots from Hawkeye, and a couple of Black Widow's bites, the Avengers backed the monsters into the portal. Thor hurled his mighty hammer, Mjolnir, at a *T. rex*, sending it stumbling back to its prehistoric world.

"Hulk has idea!" the green Avenger said as he grabbed the metal fence that surrounded a nearby baseball field.

“As long as the idea doesn’t include eating them or keeping them!” Iron Man joked.

Hulk wrapped the metal fencing around a bunch of raptors and sealed them in tight. He spun them around and around, then hurled them back into the portal, which closed in behind them. With a loud sucking noise, the portal disappeared into the air.

The Avengers had saved Central Park—and saved Iron Man and Hulk, too!

The next day, after the Avengers cleaned up the city, Tony Stark and Bruce Banner cleaned up Tony's lab.

Tony looked at Bruce and grinned. "Hey . . . wanna see who can pick up Thor's hammer or throw Cap's shield the farthest?"

Bruce shook his head. "You just don't learn your lesson, do you?" he said. Then he smiled. "Okay. Hit me!"

The Avengers' Day Off

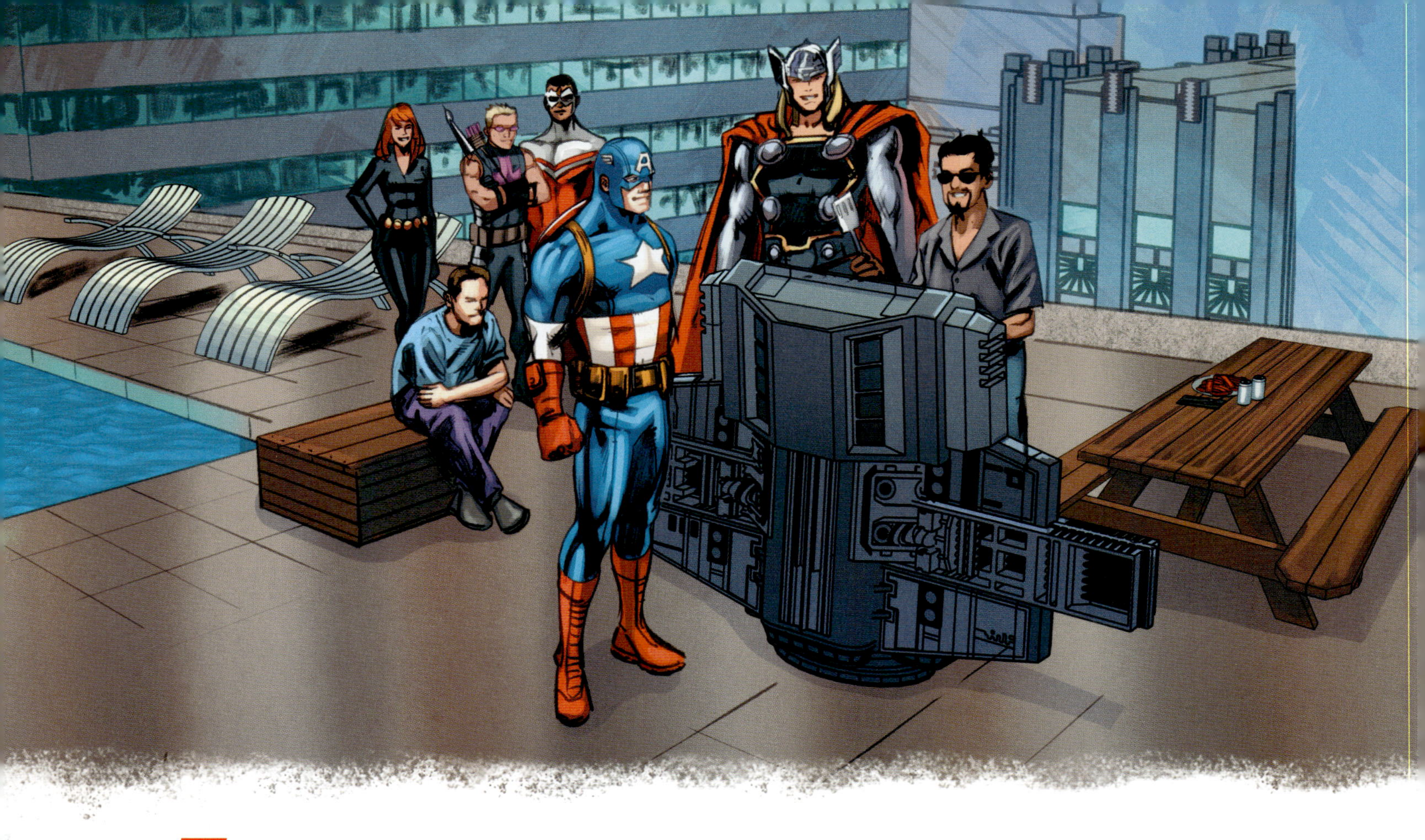

The Avengers had been battling one Super Villain after another. They'd fought Madame Hydra, Loki, and the Masters of Evil. They'd saved New York City—and the world—more times than they could count. But today was going to be different. Tony Stark had invited all the Avengers to join him atop his famous Stark Tower for a day off. With no Super Villains to fight or people to save, they were excited to do something they rarely did—relax.

"I'm not sure all of us taking off on the same day is a wise idea, Tony," Captain America said when everyone had changed out of their Super Hero uniforms. "What if we're needed?"

"Let the other heroes worry about protecting the city today," Tony said. "We need a day off."

Tony turned to Bruce Banner. "Today is a total relaxation day, especially for you. No 'Hulking out.' Now, let's eat, drink, and have some fun!"

Soon the mighty Avengers were happily eating hot dogs, hamburgers, and corn on the cob.

After lunch, the friends kicked off an intense game of volleyball. Thor did his best not to use his superstrength when serving . . . usually.

When the game was over, Tony brought his friends to the edge of the pool and told them to look down. Slowly, a solid covering rolled over the pool. "Check this out," Tony began. "The floor rolls back and forth. Below is a state-of-the-art, Olympic-sized pool—complete with rafts, bodyboards, and built-in speakers. And it's heated, of course. And above is the perfect deck!"

Tony hit a switch and the pool cover disappeared again.

"I could get used to this," Falcon said, jumping into the water. The other Avengers quickly joined him. They swam and floated and truly began to relax.

That was when the alarms sounded.

The Avengers looked at the sky. Crimson Dynamo was rocketing toward them. "This is a private party," Tony yelled.

"I'm not here as a guest," the Super Villain replied, landing with a *THUD* on the roof. Instantly, Hawkeye and Black Widow jumped out of the pool. Hawkeye ran for his bow while Black Widow took a defensive stance.

"Stop!" Tony called out. "No powers or abilities. It's our day off!"

"Your day off?" Crimson Dynamo asked, not believing what he'd just heard. "Boy, did we pick the right time to attack!"

"'We'?" Falcon asked, wondering who was with him. Just then, a massive electric spark crackled across the roof. Whiplash, with his electric whips in hand, leaped over the edge of the roof. Tony noticed Bruce Banner tensing up. "Whoa—easy, big guy!" he said.

Bruce Banner took a deep breath and tried to remain calm. But Thor had had enough. He raised his hand, signaling for Mjolnir. The magical hammer flew across the rooftop and landed in his grip, ready for action.

"Wait!" said Tony. "Put down your hammer, Thor. I've already contacted S.H.I.E.L.D. We don't need to fight them—we just need

to keep them here. We can still have our day off!"

"That's what you think!" Whiplash said. Crimson Dynamo fired blasts from his armor while Whiplash cracked his whips toward the pool, sending an electric current through the water.

The Avengers jumped out of the pool in the nick of time. Tony pressed a button and the floor began to slide back over the pool.

As the smoke cleared, Bruce's eyes began to turn green. Black Widow quickly put her hand on his shoulder. "Calm down, Bruce. Remember your training."

But Black Widow's advice didn't seem to be working.

"Imagine yourself on a peaceful beach," she continued in a calm voice as electric blasts crackled around her. "Without Super Villains," she added.

Crimson Dynamo and Whiplash intensified their attack. "The fools aren't using their powers," Crimson Dynamo yelled.

Tony turned to his friends. "I think it's time our uninvited guests enjoyed a little volleyball and a dip in the pool," he said.

Tony grabbed the volleyball net and threw it to Falcon and Hawkeye. The Avengers unfurled it and ran as wide as they could, catching both villains in the net.

"You think a mere net will stop us?" Whiplash asked.

"Well, it *is* an unbreakable net," Tony replied. "Our volleyball games can be a bit . . . intense. I didn't want the game called on account of poor equipment." He smiled.

With the villains momentarily distracted, Cap threw a Frisbee at the controls for the pool. It was a direct hit! The floor began to roll back, revealing the heated pool below.

With a loud *SPLASH*, the Super Villains fell into the giant pool.

As Crimson Dynamo and Whiplash bobbed in the water, Tony quickly hit the switch to cover the pool. "They'll be safe there until the S.H.I.E.L.D. agents arrive, which should be any minute now," he said.

Later, after Crimson Dynamo and Whiplash had been taken away, the Avengers went back to lounging by the pool.

"I'm proud of you for not using your powers to stop those chuckleheads. We took care of 'em the old-fashioned way—by outsmarting them—and we can still enjoy our day off," Tony said.

"I don't know," Bruce Banner replied. "This was a very stressful day. I think I need a day off from my day off!"

And with that, the Avengers went back to doing nothing!

Undercover Agents

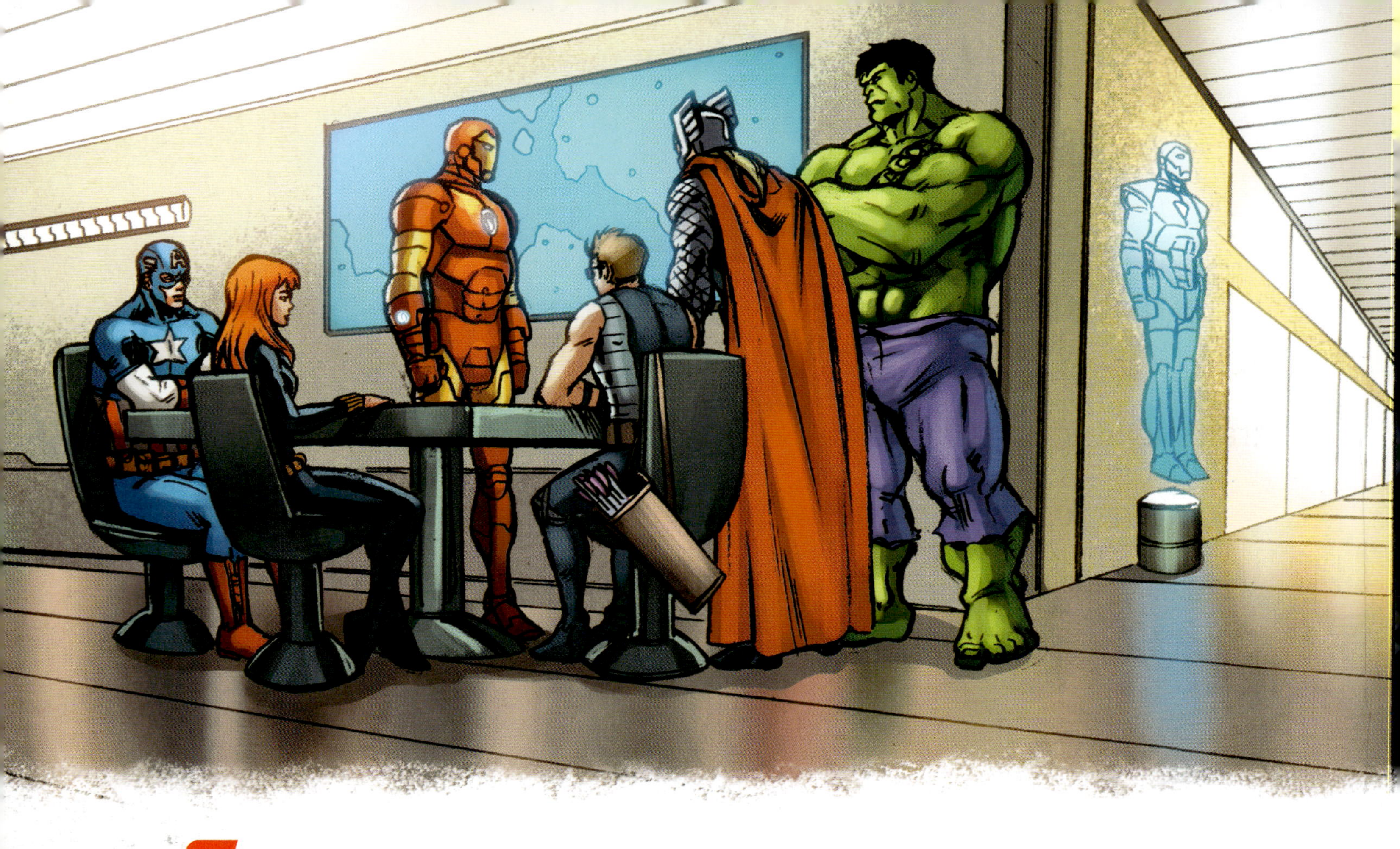

Stark Tower stood more than one hundred stories high and was filled with all kinds of high-tech gadgets and equipment. The building was named after Tony Stark, a smart and powerful businessman.

But Tony was more than just a billionaire inventor. He was also the invincible Iron Man.

One day, Iron Man called his teammates, the Avengers, to Stark Tower to discuss some troubling news.

"I have a bad feeling about *that*," Iron Man said, pointing to a building in the shadow of Stark Tower. "It seems a mysterious training academy has opened on the top floor."

Captain America stroked his chin. "What do you think it could be?"

"I don't know," Iron Man said. He pulled up an image on the computer screen. "But I spotted this man going into the building yesterday."

Black Widow studied the cloaked man on the screen. "He looks like trouble. Let's find out who he is," she said.

Cap agreed. And he had a plan: A small team of Avengers would sneak into the training academy disguised as students. Once they were in, they would find out what the mysterious man was up to.

"I'll go," said Black Widow. "I'm no stranger to combat training."

"Great," said Cap. "Take Hawkeye and Hulk with you. And good luck!"

The team was almost ready to go, but first they had to pick their disguises.

Black Widow pulled her hair back. She would pretend to be a high school teacher who wanted to learn self-defense.

Hawkeye knew just what to do. He would be an archer training for a competition.

Picking a disguise was even easier for Hulk. Nobody would ever realize that the scrawny, mild-mannered scientist Dr. Bruce Banner was really the green Goliath!

The three Avengers snuck into the training academy with ease. The guard at the front desk even scolded them for being late!

Looking the candidates over, the guard assigned their training rooms. He sent Black Widow to the self-defense training room. Hawkeye went to the archery training room. And Hulk—or rather Bruce Banner—went to a training room for beginners. The guard thought he looked too weak for advanced training!

Black Widow easily defeated her first opponent. She was a highly trained military spy, after all! But what she didn't realize was that someone was spying on her!

Elsewhere in the training academy, the cloaked figure watched Black Widow's performance. "Those moves look very familiar," the man said, narrowing his eyes. Suddenly, he jumped up. "I know where I've seen those moves before. I've fought against them. That's Black Widow! But what is she doing here?"

The mysterious man opened the door to Black Widow's training room.

Black Widow knew it was the man from the photo, but something else about him seemed familiar.

"You have great moves," he said. "Let's see how you do against me!"

They fought back and forth, but he was always one step ahead of her. She soon realized he was using her own moves against her!

How can this be? she thought with alarm. *There's only one person who can mimic my moves, and that's*—"Taskmaster!" she said as he pulled off his hood. She had to warn the others.

Black Widow ducked under the Taskmaster's punch and slid away from him. She quickly found Hawkeye in the archery room. The two ran to find Bruce, but the Taskmaster had beaten them there.

"Increase the level of training to advanced," he told his guards. "If the Avengers want a fight, I'll give them a fight!"

“I wouldn’t get him angry if I were you,” Black Widow said.

“And why not?” the Taskmaster questioned. “Your friend has no chance!”

But it was too late. As the Taskmaster’s forces attacked Bruce Banner, the scientist covered his face and screamed. Everyone in the room retreated as they saw his back expand and tear through his shirt. He grew several feet taller, and his hands became huge!

“It’s . . . it’s Hulk!” the Taskmaster cried, watching the giant smash his training robots.

Black Widow smiled and shrugged. “I told you not to get him mad!”

As the three Avengers battled the Taskmaster’s goons, the sneaky Super Villain pulled out a bow that looked just like Hawkeye’s and shot a cable arrow to a nearby building. Then he slid down the line to the roof, making his escape.

"We need to get back to Stark Tower and fill in the other Avengers!" Black Widow cried.

Hawkeye smiled. "I know what to do," he said. He tied a rope to one of his arrows and fired it all the way to the roof of Stark Tower. Then he gave the other end of the rope to Hulk. "If the Taskmaster can do it, so can I!" he yelled. Hulk nodded. While Black Widow and Hawkeye held on to him, he jumped off the building and slid down the line to Stark Tower.

"Well, at least we know who's behind the training academy," Captain America said as they gathered around the table once more.

"It's the Taskmaster, all right," Black Widow said. "He figured out who we were, but now he knows we're on to him."

Captain America nodded. "By the way, how did you get out after he discovered you?"

Hawkeye and Black Widow looked at Hulk and smiled.

"Oh, we make a smashing team!"

What Goes Up Must Come Down

One sunny morning in New York, Captain America decided to visit the Statue of Liberty. But time off doesn't last long when you're an Avenger, and he soon found himself called to action by the sound of screams!

"Look! Over there!" a tourist shouted, pointing across the water to Manhattan. Bicycles, cars, and even people were flying into the air!

No bridge connected Liberty Island to the rest of Manhattan, and Cap didn't have time to wait for the next ferry. Using his communicator, he contacted his good friend and fellow Avenger Falcon.

"Where to, Cap?" asked the winged Avenger, carrying Captain America across the water.

"Times Square, Falcon. I'm guessing the rest of the Avengers could probably use our help."

Captain America was right. The Avengers had their hands full, trying to rescue people from gravity gone wild!

As tourists floated into the sky, Hawkeye shot arrows attached to nets and anchored people to the tops of lampposts. Meanwhile, Hulk used his incredible strength to keep a bus filled with people from drifting into the air!

The airborne members of the Avengers did their part to save people, too.

"This is madness!" shouted Iron Man. "We can't rescue everyone!"

"But that won't stop us from trying!" exclaimed Captain America as he and Falcon arrived on the scene.

"What—or who—could be behind this?" asked Falcon.

"This seems most familiar," said Thor. "Perhaps it is the work of—"

Before Thor could finish his thought, the face of the evil scientist Graviton appeared on one of Times Square's giant video screens.

"People of New York," the speakers blared, "I am Graviton. I do not wish to harm you. I seek only those costumed do-gooders who sent me to prison: the Avengers!"

Graviton had once been a brilliant scientist named Franklin Hall. An accident had given him control over gravity, which was why he had renamed himself Graviton. The Avengers had stopped him many times in the past. Now he had escaped from prison and was out for revenge.

"My demands are simple," Graviton continued. "Either the Avengers surrender themselves to me at noon today, or I will send the island of Manhattan and the Statue of Liberty into space!

"Noon," Graviton repeated. "And not a minute later."

With that, the screens went blank and gravity slowly returned to normal.

"We can't surrender!" exclaimed Hawkeye. "Graviton will just take us prisoner and go ahead with his plans anyway!"

Iron Man agreed. "You're right. We can't trust Graviton, but he'll do tremendous harm if we don't give him what he wants."

The armored Avenger paused. "I have a plan," he said at last. "*We* can't surrender," Iron Man explained. "But *you* can."

Iron Man pointed at Captain America, Hawkeye, and Black Widow!

At noon, Captain America, Hawkeye, and Black Widow surrendered to Graviton, who used his powers to keep anyone else from coming near them.

"I never thought any of you would surrender," he gloated. Then he added, "But embarrassing you Avengers was just the beginning. . . .

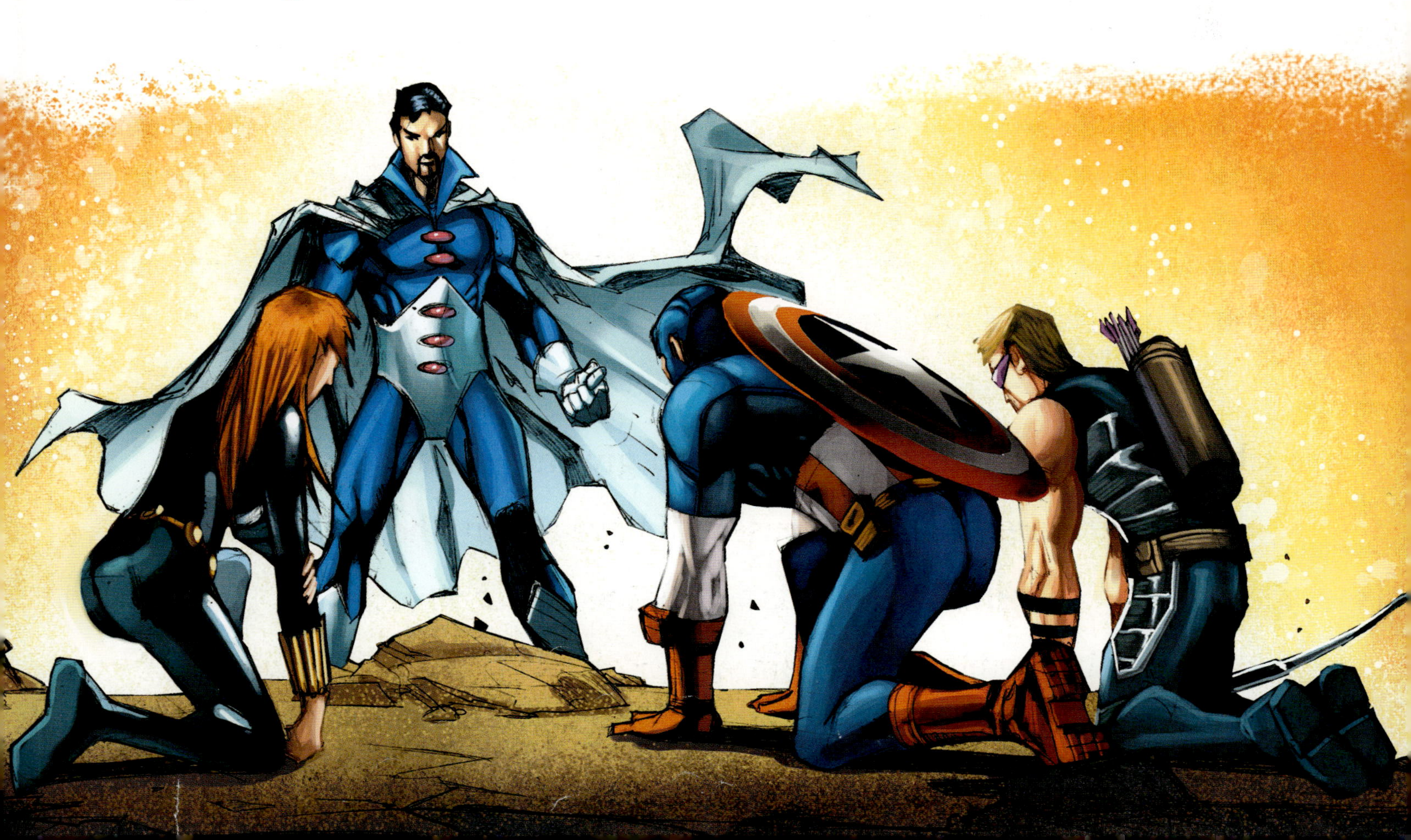

"The real prize is the billion-dollar ransom I'll get for the island of Manhattan!" Graviton continued.

Suddenly, the Avengers felt the ground lurch beneath them, and the entire island of Manhattan floated into the air! To the south, the Statue of Liberty rose off its base!

Cap threw his shield at the villain, knocking him unconscious.

As quickly as Manhattan had risen, it started to drop! Luckily, Iron Man's plan was already working.

"Graviton was boasting so much he never saw your shield coming," Black Widow said. "Thor, Iron Man . . . Graviton is down. You're up!"

High in the sky, the mighty Thor whirled his Asgardian hammer, Mjolnir, over his head, summoning storm clouds and creating an enormous rainstorm. "I shall not let you down," he told Black Widow. "Creating storms such as this is child's play. The wind and rain shall raise the sea level, slowing the isle of Manhattan's fall back to Earth—"

Suddenly, Iron Man interrupted on his communicator!

"As long as I do the hard part!" Iron Man said, laughing as he flew circles around the island at high speed to turn Thor's storm waters into a cushion to gently lower the island back into place.

"We're all going to have a lot of repair work to do when this is over, Tony," Cap reminded his fellow Avenger.

"Speaking of repairs," added Iron Man, "Falcon, how's Lady Liberty?"

"Not to worry," Falcon replied. "She's holding up just fine, but you might want to hurry. . . ."

Hulk groaned as he held up the Statue of Liberty to keep it from smashing into the island beneath it.

Hulk had leaped to Liberty Island in time to catch the falling statue. Straining under the weight, but not letting any harm come to the symbol of freedom, Hulk shouted, “Other Avengers better come fix lady statue soon! Hulk love to smash . . . but Hulk hate lifting!”

An Unexpected Hero

Agent Phil Coulson was in his office aboard S.H.I.E.L.D.'s top secret plane when a call came in from his boss, Nick Fury.

"I'm sending you to Egypt, Coulson," Fury said. "There are strange signals coming from some long-abandoned ruins, and I need you to check it out."

Coulson nodded. "I'll have the plane change course at once," he replied.

Coulson arrived at the ruins and turned on the plane's scanners. Something was *definitely* wrong. The energy readings were off the charts!

Coulson carefully approached the ruins. Hidden behind a pile of bricks was a strange door.

Coulson walked through the door and looked around. He expected to see a dusty tomb or a library of old scrolls. Instead, he found a high-tech lab!

Agent Coulson studied the unusual equipment. “These systems are so advanced!” he exclaimed. “I’ve never seen anything like them.”

“That’s because *I* invented them,” a voice said. It was Ultron.

"Welcome, Agent Coulson," Ultron said with a laugh. "I was hoping you would join me."

Agent Coulson backed up. He was trapped! The robotic Super Villain was blocking the only exit.

"I don't know what you're planning, Ultron," Coulson began, "but—"

Suddenly, Coulson stopped talking. Ultron had thrown a disc at him that made him freeze in place.

In New York, the Avengers were finishing a battle against A.I.M., a group of evil scientists bent on ruling the world.

"Come on, guys. A doom ray?" taunted Iron Man. "How unimaginative. I thought you A.I.M. guys would do better than that!"

Just then, a large figure appeared in the sky above the Avengers.

"Isn't that your Hulkbuster armor?" Falcon asked Iron Man. Iron Man had designed a special armor that was as tough as Hulk himself.

"Ha," sneered Hulk. "Puny armor. Hulk is strongest one there is!"

"We know that, big guy," Iron Man assured Hulk. "But that *is* one of my suits. What's it doing here?"

Before anyone could answer, the Hulkbuster armor suddenly attacked!

"Look out!" Captain America cried, raising his shield.

The Hulkbuster landed, and Thor ripped off its helmet. Inside was a gagged Agent Coulson.

Iron Man removed the gag. "What are you doing in my suit?" he asked the agent.

"Ultron froze me with some strange disc and then shoved me inside," Coulson explained. "I've been trapped in here for hours!"

“Don’t worry, Coulson, we’ll get you out of there,” Iron Man assured the agent. “I just need to get you back to my armory. Hulk?”

Hulk grunted and picked up the suit. With Coulson over his shoulder, he followed the other Avengers to Iron Man’s armory. Inside were all the suits Iron Man had created over the years.

Iron Man plugged Coulson and the Hulkbuster armor into his computer. Almost immediately, a loud alarm started to sound.

"The armor uploaded some kind of computer virus into the armory's systems!" Iron Man cried.

"That's right, Stark!" a voice announced. It was Ultron! He had followed Coulson back to New York and all the way to Iron Man's armory.

"You fools are so predictable," Ultron said. "I knew you would bring your agent here to free him."

Iron Man walked to a control panel and pushed a button. Nothing happened.

Ultron laughed. "My virus is in your computer system," he said. "Your armory belongs to me!"

Ultron raised his arms and Iron Man's collection of spare suits rose into the air.

"And now, Avengers, let's see how you do against not one, but an *army* of Iron Men," screamed Ultron.

The empty suits surrounded the heroes. Then, at Ultron's command, they attacked!

From inside the Hulkbuster, Agent Coulson watched the Avengers battle the empty suits.

I wish I could be out there, fighting with them, he thought.

"These mere empty shells cannot defeat us," proclaimed Thor as he pounded one of the heavier suits with his hammer.

"Especially not when we work together!" agreed Captain America. "Avengers, assemble!"

Working together, the Avengers broke apart one suit after another.

"You see, Ultron?" asked Iron Man. "Even when we're outnumbered, the Avengers will always defeat evil!"

But Ultron just laughed. "Once again, you did just as I had hoped. Thank you for saving me the trouble of breaking these suits apart myself!"

Ultron raised his arms again, and the pieces of armor that were scattered throughout the room flew toward him! One by one, the pieces attached to his metal body—making him bigger, stronger, and more powerful than ever!

"Behold *Mega-Ultron*," shouted Ultron, "the greatest robot of all time!"

The Avengers battled bravely against the new, improved Ultron—but he was too strong. "I can't believe it," cried Hawkeye. "Even with all of us fighting him, he's still winning!"

Behind them, unnoticed, Iron Man's computer continued to work. Suddenly, there was a faint *click* and the Hulkbuster armor popped open.

Agent Coulson reached into the armor and picked up the disc Ultron had used to freeze him. "Maybe I can use Ultron's own plan against him," he said.

With Ultron distracted, Coulson climbed the armor racks to a spot above the giant robot. Then, taking a deep breath, he leaped toward Ultron.

Coulson reached out with the disc and—

BAM! The disc attached to Ultron, who instantly froze in place!

"Smart thinking, son of Coul," Thor said. "You tricked Ultron. Very Loki of you!"

"I'm glad I was able to help," said Coulson, pleased.

"If you want to help, come up here and get all these pieces off Ultron!" shouted Iron Man. "I hope you're good at jigsaw puzzles, because we need to fix *all* of my suits!"

As he helped put together the Iron Man suits, Coulson smiled. He was proud to fight beside the Avengers and call them friends.

The End

page 60
page 101
page 59
page 67
page 83
page 107
page 133
page 198